In Dreams: The Very Short Stories of

**Ryūnosuke Akutagawa**

*Translated from the Japanese by Ryan Choi*

PAPER + INK

**In Dreams: The Very Short Stories of Ryūnosuke Akutagawa**

*Selected and Translated from the Japanese by Ryan Choi*

This edition has been published in 2023
in the United Kingdom by Paper + Ink.

**www.paperand.ink**
Twitter: @paper_andink
Instagram: paper_and.ink

1 2 3 4 5 6 7 8 9 10

ISBN 9781911475569

A CIP catalogue record for this book is available from the British Library.

Jacket design by James Nunn: www.jamesnunn.co.uk | @Gnunkse

Printed and bound in Great Britain.

The author gratefully acknowledges the following publications, in which some of the translated texts in this volume first appeared in different form:

*Asymptote, The Best Small Fictions 2019, Chicago Review, Columbia, EPOCH, Gulf Coast, Harper's Magazine, Hotel, Indiana Review, The Iowa Review, jubilat, New England Review, New York Tyrant, River Styx, The Rupture, The Shanghai Literary Review, The Southern Review, Tin House, Two Lines, The Wigleaf Top 50 2019 and The Yale Review.*

"The Parrot: Notes on the Great Earthquake" first appeared in *Pets: An Anthology* (New York: New York Tyrant Books, 2020).

# CONTENTS

# IN DREAMS

It's said that seeing colour in dreams is a sign of exhausted nerves. But ever since I was a child, my dreams have been rich with colour. I can't believe there's even such a thing as a colourless dream. The other day, I had a dream in which I saw the poet H. K. at the seaside baths. He had on a hat of barley straw and a beautiful navy-blue cloak. I was so taken with the blue that I asked if he could tell me what it was called.

"This?" the poet said whimsically, staring at the sand. "Why, this is the colour of *Sapporo* ..."

I have even heard it said on occasion that smells aren't experienced in dreams. But I can recall a dream I had in which my nose was piqued by the odour of burning rubber. It was sunset, and I was walking in a remote town that had a river from which the odour seemed to emanate. I could see alligators as hefty as logs swimming in the water, and the whole time while walking, I kept thinking to myself, *Is this the way to the Suez Canal?*

(Actually, this is the only dream I can recall in which smell played a central role.)

Sometimes in my dreams I also compose haiku and songs. Nothing first-rate has ever taken shape, but at the moment of conception I firmly believe in the merit of my creations. Four or five days ago, I had a dream in which I was standing on a path in the middle of a field in the countryside. Not far from me was a congregation of men and women, and the people in the centre were carrying a shrine on their shoulders together and shouting, "Heave ho! Heave ho!"

I was inspired to commemorate the scene in a haiku, which I intoned to myself several times, feeling that I was a poetic genius. In the morning, when I woke up and tried to remember the poem, I was appalled by the junk my memory dredged up:

*On tiptoes, I watch the passing of a shrine.*

*Undated*

# LASTING IMPRESSION

I recently accepted a commission to write about the mountain town of Ikaho, despite having spent only one night there during high school, on a hiking trip with two friends up Mount Myōgi and Mount Akagi. I recall little about the town itself, and even less about its famed views and hot springs. I have but a vague memory of riding a rickety train up the mountainside and being uneasy about the rusted tracks webbed with bush and vine, and the lack of straps to hold on to.

After arriving in town, we found a room at a nondescript inn. There we happened to meet a sophisticated, middle-aged man who was staying in the room by ours. He was, by his eager admission, a regular at these hot springs, claiming they possessed special powers of rejuvenation that were the secret to his youthful appearance. We accompanied him to the hot springs no fewer than six times the following day, and after our last bath our bodies were so withered we could barely steady ourselves for the walk back. The halls of the inn seemed to elongate and twist before us, and I remember nearly fainting.

Once we had settled in our rooms, we all found that we were mysteriously unable to relax. As soon as the sun set, the four of us packed our bags, checked out, and trekked over to Takasaki Station, where my friends and I were embarrassed to discover that we couldn't afford our fares to Ueno – we had spent too much money on the hot springs and the inn. We confessed our predicament to the man, who, with no hesitation, gifted us one hundred and twenty *sen*, then bid us farewell.

As I said above, I have but a vague memory of Ikaho and its majestic waterfalls and valleys; whenever the topic of its renowned hot springs comes up, I think of this man we met, and how each time we soaked in the waters together he carried on at nauseating length about his plans to design and manufacture a compact, one-seat automobile and become one of the country's wealthiest men. Just today in the papers, I read an article about the invention of a two-seat automobile, and began to wonder about the man – for I have yet to read about a one-seat automobile being made.

*August 1919*

# DUCK HUNTING

The last time I saw Professor Keigetsu Ōmachi was in 1924, on New Year's Day, when we went duck hunting in Shinagawa Bay with a group of friends – Misei Kosugi, Taneaki Shindai, and Torayoshi Ichikawa. We met early that morning at the boathouse near Ichi-no Bridge in Honjō, and from there we coasted down the river on our rented boat loaded with a day's worth of supplies. Kosugi and Shindai were both seasoned hunters, and it showed in their confidence and poise, the quality of their gear, and their style of dress. To make matters worse (I'm highly self-conscious), the guide they hired was an eminent hunter himself, whose name is still known to hunters today. In retrospect, the great irony of all this was that, even with these hunters in attendance, none of us shot any birds that day. Cormorants and ducks alike, on every one of our approaches, spotted our boat without fail and scattered into the sky before we could take aim.

Professor Ōmachi was amused no end at our repeated failures to bag a feathered prize, clapping his hands and laughing whenever a flock dispersed and settled at a distance.

"Amazing!" he remarked. "The ducks are literate. Look! They flee to the areas marked NO HUNTING. They know exactly where to go."

To everyone's dismay, throughout the entire outing, Ōmachi's obnoxious comments blared from beneath his booze-soaked moustache, and the wide-spread hood of his fox-brown hat cast an ominous shadow on the waters around the boat. The spectacle of Ōmachi alone was enough to frighten the ducks away.

Thus we spent a total of ten hours on the bay drifting in the wind, with nothing to show for it at the end of the day. By the time we returned to the docks, Ōmachi, who had been revelling so garrulously in our misadventure, had sobered up and was now in a sullen mood. As we disembarked, he spoke up in a downcast voice:

"I promised my children I would bring home two ducks, one for each of them. I don't know what to do now, I can't let them down. They're planning to give the ducks to their teachers tomorrow as gifts."

After discussing it outside the boathouse, we decided to walk to a nearby poultry shop where Ōmachi could buy a pair of ducks. The only problem, Kosugi pointed out after Ōmachi had made his purchase, was that these ducks had been captured with birdlime traps. "That means," he said, "there's no bullet holes in them. Don't you think your kids will notice? We ought to shoot each of them once, so it looks like they were hunted with rifles. Come on. Let's do it in the alley over there."

Ōmachi shook his head like a timorous child. "No, they're fine as is," he said, wrapping the birdlimed ducks in old newspapers. "My children won't notice the difference." When he was finished, he said goodbye to us curtly, then carried the bundles home, one under each arm.

*Undated*

# SNOW

On an overcast winter day, I was riding the Chuō train out west, gazing at the mountain range framed in the window of my carriage. The mountains were enveloped in a pure white that resembled mountain *skin* more than snow. As I stared at the lofty peaks, a peculiar scene from my past came to mind:

Four or five years ago, on a similarly overcast winter day, I was visiting an artist friend of mine at his studio. It was heated by a flaking cast-iron stove, and the walls were decorated sparely with a curation of his oils. I was conversing with him and one of his models, who happened to be there sitting for a portrait. The model was beautiful. She looked like she had a touch of foreign blood in her veins, a trait which her bob cut hair and cigarette smoking did much to accentuate. At one point, I noticed through a rift in the smoke that her eyelashes had all been recently tweezed.

When our conversation shifted to the severe cold that year, my friend talked about how the soil in his garden changed character from season to season – and particularly how it felt during winter.

"What I mean to say is, soil is a living creature with seasons too," he said. "No different from you and me."

After ending his aside, he filled his pipe with tobacco, tamped it with his thumb and studied our faces. I had nothing to add, and blankly took a sip of my coffee, which had turned lukewarm and scentless. My friend's words seemed to affect the model, however; her swollen eyelids arched pensively. Looking off into the distance while exhaling a ring of smoke, she said:

"It's the same with skin. I used to have beautiful skin before I got into this line of work. Now, every year, my skin only gets more cracked and wrinkled ..."

On that overcast winter day, riding the Chuō train out west, I gazed at the mountain range framed in the window of my carriage. The mountains were enveloped in a pure white that resembled coarse human skin more than snow. As I stared at those lofty peaks, I was reminded of the words of that Japanese model with the foreign blood in her veins, and not a single eyelash to her name.

*April 1925*

# A CASE OF TWO FAKES

Last summer, I received a letter from Yamagata Prefecture. The sender's name was "Misao Yamazaki". I had never met or corresponded with this person before, so I was alarmed to read that he was awaiting repayment from me on a 100-*yen* loan, and was on the verge of pursuing legal action because of my delinquency. According to the letter, I had been lodging at the Harikyū Inn in Sendai when I had contacted him about the loan, and, because of my fame, he had wired the money.

I have never been to Sendai, let alone the Harikyū Inn.

As the letter had been sent by contents-certified post, I replied in kind, asserting that the man was unknown to me and that I had no memory of borrowing this money. Then I departed for Karuizawa, forgetting about the mix-up.

Some weeks later, a second letter from Misao Yamazaki reached me in Karuizawa, forwarded from my Tokyo address. This one came by standard post, but its contents were identical, if blunter in tone: I definitely had borrowed the 100 *yen*, and

I had better pay it back. It also surfaced that Misao Yamazaki was not a man but a woman – and in very ill health. Naturally, I felt awful upon reading this, but on principle I had no intention of being charitable, and was still aggrieved at being nagged about a debt I had not incurred. I wrote back, reiterating my lack of memory about the loan, and suggested that before she pursue legal action, she would do well to look into whether the "Ryūnosuke Akutagawa" to whom she had wired money was the real me, and not some imposter who had ripped her off.

After that, there were no more letters from Misao Yamazaki. Around this time, however, I happened to receive a letter from an inn at the Iizaka Onsen in Fukushima. According to this one, someone there ran up a tab under my name, and the inn was demanding that it be paid.

Now that I think about it, even before these two incidents, I had had another experience involving a letter of dubious origin, written sincerely but based on lies. It was from a man in Nagano Prefecture expressing condolences for a burglary that supposedly had happened at my home. I didn't recognize his name – or the burglary – but at the end of the letter he thanked me for writing the preface to his book, which I had never heard of before.

(Needless to say, I had no memory of writing the preface either.) Because the letter had no return address, I couldn't send a reply.

As it happens, I'm not alone in having these experiences. Recently, I've been hearing lots of stories about famous artists and writers having their names abused. My warning to all lovers of art and books: *be on guard; imposters abound.*

Fake painters and poets are easy to expose: have them paint or write a poem in your presence, and they will out themselves. It's the fake fiction writers who are more elusive. In person, there's less to judge in terms of performance.

In any case, take it from me: it's misguided to watch a fiction writer at work in the hope of catching their secrets. It's like watching an elephant in a zoo.

# JUN'ICHIRŌ TANIZAKI

One early summer afternoon I was in Kanda, book browsing with Jun'ichirō Tanizaki. He was dressed, of all things, in a jet-black suit and a flashy red tie knotted snugly around his neck – proof of his romantic temperament. Everyone we passed in the street, man and woman alike, paused to stare; based on the looks they gave, I was sure they all had the same impression as I had. But when I pointed this out to Tanizaki, he denied it angrily.

"They're looking at you, not me," he said. "Why are you wearing that thing, anyway?"

Instead of my light summer jacket, I had on my father's heavy winter coat, the sort that a Buddhist priest or tea ceremony teacher would wear with their kimono at all times of year – in other words, hardly an uncommon sight. It was Tanizaki who was attracting all the stares, with his outré tie that looked like a crimson rose. But I didn't expect to persuade him of this truth, irrefutable though it was: he suffered, as I did, from the poet's disdain for reason.

If the two of us agreed on anything, it was that it was hot and we were thirsty. We went into a café in the backstreets of Jinbōchō, where we ordered a round of sodas and then fell into a silence – loudened only by Tanizaki's red tie, that beacon of romantic zealotry to which my eyes could not but stick. When the waitress, whose face powder was marred in spots, arrived with our cups in hand, the bubbles danced on the water's surface, as lucid as only truth can be. I'll never forget what she said to Tanizaki after she set down our cups, lingering with her hand pressed to the table, her eyes bewitched by the red tie.

"The colour is unbelievable!" she said, almost giddily. "I can't stop staring at your tie!"

Ten minutes later, as we were about to leave, I took a fifty-*sen* bill out of my wallet to tip the waitress. Unsurprisingly, Tanizaki – who, like every Tokyo native, was opposed to tipping – scoffed at me. "Put that away," he said, pushing the money toward me. "She didn't go out of her way. And she's already being paid."

In the past, I would have deferred to Tanizaki, owing to his seniority; but this time I didn't, and left the crumpled bill on the table. I couldn't have disagreed with him more than I did at that moment. Our waitress had not only brought our drinks, but also validated for me the truth of his red tie. As a matter of fact, to this day, that crumpled fifty-*sen* bill ranks as the most earnest tip I've ever given.

# A GAME OF TAG

A boy was playing tag with a girl on the backroads of their neighbourhood. It was late afternoon, but still bright out. The gas lamps were beginning to glow.

"Catch me if you can!" the boy said, nimbly skirting the younger girl's reach. When he turned to wag his tongue at her, he found himself fixated instead on a strange, grave frown on her face, which lodged itself in his memory for months and then years, before fading.

Two decades later, on a night train bound for snow country, the boy ran into the girl again, and they recognized each other immediately, though she was now a woman and he was a man. The scent of damp shoes and coats engulfed them both, and awakened old memories. "It's been a while," he said with a cigarette between his lips, staring in disbelief at his childhood friend.

The woman mentioned her recently deceased husband and spoke fondly of her parents and siblings. The man confided that he and his comrades had been in prison until three days earlier. Observing her face as they spoke, he saw her expression briefly contort into that grave frown of old, and suddenly he felt like a boy of twelve again, immersed in their game of tag at sunset.

Today, the boy and girl are husband and wife, and live in a house outside the city, where the husband still watches his wife's face for her frown ... but always for naught.

*1926*

# MERCHANT VIRGIN MARY

*Under siege, the inner grounds of Hara Castle, under the sway of the Catholic rebel leader Amakusa Shirō. Explosions and flames, arrows and bullets winging over mounds of the dead and the living. An old man lies in raptures, singing hallelujah before a portrait of the Virgin Mary hanging on a stone wall. Mortally wounded by bullets, he will never stand again. Under the anointing gaze of his white-robed saviour, he gives himself unto death ...*

I saw this portrait once during a visit to Hara Castle. I can confirm that the person in the painting is not the Virgin Mary, but a plain, redheaded woman in a white dress, the type who's fond of roses. Beneath the portrait, there are the words in golden Roman script:

WILHELM TOBACCO COMPANY. AMSTERDAM, HOLLAND.

*Undated*

# PAGODA TREES

I was at an *itchūbushi* concert listening to a performance of *The Stone Pillow* when I began thinking about pagoda trees. I'm not nearly as learned on the subject of these fabled trees as a classical vocalist must be, studying a piece for years before mounting the stage with their *shamisen*. All my knowledge about pagoda trees comes from overhearing, in childhood, the voice lessons that my parents took. As I learned it from them, the pagoda tree in literature appears as far back as the *sūtras* of the bodhisattva Guanyin: *"Time passes in the garden. The crowns of pagoda trees."*

In *The Stone Pillow*, an old woman welcomes a weary traveller into her home in order to steal his money. After he falls asleep with his head on the eponymous stone pillow, the woman sneaks into the room, crushes his head with a rope-lashed stone, then steals his money. The following day, a second visitor shows up at her door. This time, it's a beautiful boy who asks to stay the night. The old woman welcomes him inside, planning to kill and rob him, too. After the boy retires to his room, she sneaks in with the rope-lashed stone and crushes his head on the stone pillow – only to find her daughter instead, lying dead on the bed. The boy then manifests before the woman as the Bodhisattva Guanyin, chanting a ballad about karmic retribution. (Unbeknownst to the woman, her precious daughter had fallen in love with the boy at first sight, and had crept into his bed after dark.)

Today there's a body of water known as "Old Lady Lake" on the grounds of Sensō Temple in Asakusa, Tokyo. This is, reputedly, the lake in which the old woman drowned herself with the infamous stone.

My lasting fascination with *The Stone Pillow*, which I can't claim for *Black Hair* or *Eight Yoshiwara Scenes*, can be traced back to when I saw the early woodblock prints by Kuniyoshi that are based on the story. I was mesmerized then by Kuniyoshi's depiction of Guanyin's clothes, his Western-style brushstrokes, and for the longest time, whenever I saw a pagoda tree, I would marvel at how precisely Kuniyoshi's woodblock prints mirrored the patterns of branches and leaves.

Then, four or five years ago, when I was travelling through Peking, I became sick of pagoda trees all at once. Everywhere

I went, they were a persistent eyesore. What began as a poetic vista, for me, ended in tasteless excess. Nowadays, the only thing I find attractive about pagoda trees are the shells of their unripe beans.

*Peking: Tapping ash on the road. The shells of pagoda trees.*

*October 1926*

# THE HERON AND THE MANDARIN DUCK

This happened one summer, two or three years ago. I was walking through the bustle of Ginza when I spotted a pair of women walking ahead of me. They were beautiful – but not by any means your average beauties. Their figures were more conspicuous and clashing than any I've seen side by side. One, whom I shall call the Heron, was long-necked and willowy, while the other had an unorthodox physique needing more words to do it justice. In China, since ancient times, the ideal female figure has been depicted in paintings as tall and lithe, famously epitomized by the Han Empress Zhao Feiyan, who is traditionally contrasted with the no less august Yang Guifei, the plump concubine of the Tang Emperor Xuanzong. The Heron's companion, who was more than a bit fleshy, unquestionably fell into this rarefied latter class, as her size enhanced her impeccably proportioned frame, which she guided along in her stroll with an opulent roll of her hips, reminiscent of the mandarin duck's sashay. The women were dressed identically, with spiffy silk sashes ribboning the waists of their kimonos, which were striped and printed with miniature red fawns. When I saw that even their parasols were the same (sheathed in those reticulated sleeves that were the season's rage – now all but obsolete), I suspected that they were sisters. As I trailed them, poring over every aspect of their bodies, gestures, and clothes as if they were models on a pedestal, I thought of a jingle that has haunted the pages of women's magazines for the better part of thirty years: *In summer, thinly clad, female shapes for all to see.*

With this jingle in my ear, I passed by the women to get a look at their faces, glimpsing their hair, arranged in spade-shaped braids, and seeing their faces up close, though fleetingly, I felt positive that they were sisters, each about twenty years old, and judged – not confidently – that the beauty of the Mandarin Duck was ever so slightly inferior to that of the Heron.

Once they were behind me I forgot about them, and continued on my aimless walk. As I have said, all this happened on a bustling street in Ginza on a scorching summer day. That those two beauties slipped so swiftly from my mind, I believe, was not because I lack the aesthetic impressionability of a poet, but rather because I was consumed with battling the blindingly golden summer heat, dabbing my sweat with a handkerchief and fanning myself with my straw hat.

Not more than ten minutes later, I was in my seat on the train about to depart Ginza- yonchōme when the pair scurried aboard just as the doors were closing. Although the carriage wasn't crowded, the only free seat happened to be the one to my right. The Heron, with the presumption of an older sister, plopped herself down into it as the Mandarin Duck stood by timidly, gripping the strap. I opened my book and set out to slog through the swelteringly dense biography of Mahatma Gandhi – though, in truth, I couldn't focus, much less absorb a single page of this tome, which I could now only think about conquering someday. The train then started with a jolt, and the Mandarin Duck momentarily lost her footing. I quickly stood and offered my seat to her in exceedingly gentlemanly fashion, and before either sister could thank me, I dashed into the neighbouring carriage.

The fact that someone like me, an avowed egotist, would commit this seeming act of chivalry was not a chance anomaly: only seconds before, to my horror, having glanced up at the Mandarin Duck, I saw, peeking from her nostrils, bushes of thick, wiry hair; and the Heron, too, had a grungy air about her, with sour-smelling locks like she hadn't washed for weeks. As if that weren't enough, the topic of their boisterous chatter was menstrual cycles: the quirks of their own and those of the women they knew.

Unhappily for me, ever since this incident, the jingle, *In summer, thinly clad, female shapes for all to see* has become a haunting symbol of disillusionment, a call to precaution in judgments of beauty. No matter how divine the Heron and the Mandarin Duck first appeared on that Ginza day, I could never extol them as great – or even middling – beauties. At the very least, before I can think of bestowing such praise on anyone, my nose must have its say.

*June 1924*

# FROGS

Surrounded by frogs, I lay by the old pond, its rim grown thick with cattails and reeds, above whose tips the trimmed heads of the poplar trees on the roadside rustled below the clouds glazed like polished glass. Reflected in the pond, this summer scene was imbued with silent beauty, more potent than summer itself.

Initially, the croaking of the frogs sounded like nonsense – until I listened to them carefully and realized their croaks were not gibberish, but words in a fierce debate. By no means is it a fable to say that Aesop's talking frogs still exist ...

One frog came to dominate the rest. Perched on the highest leaf of the tallest reed, he pontificated in the manner of a professor: "And why does the water exist? The water exists for us to swim in!" he proclaimed. "And why do the insects exist? The insects exist for us to eat!"

"Hear! Hear!" boomed the frogs, who were so plenteous that the pond and the scene reflected in it trembled, and the serpent napping in the branches of a poplar awoke, rearing its head and licking its lips. Groggily, it turned its eyes on the pond, then fell back asleep.

The professor continued: "And why does the soil exist? The soil exists for the plants and trees to grow in. And why do the plants and trees exist? They exist to give frogs shade on sunny days. There is only one conclusion to make. All the Earth exists for our sake, the great frog race!"

"*Hear! Hear!*" boomed the frogs.

At this second round of cheers the serpent woke again, and its black eyes flickered wrathfully. It cracked its body like a whip and slithered down the tree, then through the reeds toward the pond where the professor's voice swelled grandiosely: "And why do the heavens above the Earth exist? They exist for the sun to shine in. And why does the sun exist? It exists to dry our backs when we get wet. Therefore, all the heavens exist for our sake, and if all of the water and the plants and the trees and the insects and the soil and the sun exist for our sake, then there is only one conclusion to make: all of the *universe* exists for our sake! It was created for us, the great frog race! Let us give thanks and praise to the Great Frog! *Praise!*"

And the professor looked skyward, eyes rolling round in his sockets, and said again: "Praise the Great Frog! *Praise* –"

And the serpent lunged forward and gulped him down, then slithered off into the reeds. The hysteria that ensued was unparalleled in the history of the great frog race.

*<Ribbit!> "No!"*

*<Croak!> "Why!"*

*"Our leader is gone!" <Ribbit!> <Croak!>*

A young frog cried out amongst the sobbing masses: "And if the water and the plants and the trees and the insects and the soil and the heavens and the sun exist for our sake, then what about the serpent ... does the serpent exist for our sake, too?"

After a moment, a voice said: "Yes, the serpent exists for our sake. If the serpent never ate us, the pond would become too full, and we would run out of food. Those eaten by the serpent should be venerated as saints who have given their lives for the great frog race. Yes, the serpent exists for our sake; everything in the universe exists for our sake. We must go on praising the Great Frog. Praise ..."

This was the wisdom of an elder frog.

*September 1917*

# KIMONO

I had a dream –

There was a party in a restaurant's grand banquet room. The guests were wearing either Japanese or Western clothes, depending on their tastes. More than adornments for the body, everyone's choice of dress was the subject of a raucously frank group discussion.

"Your frock is dated, don't you think? I bet it was tailored back when naturalism was the craze."

"I'm impressed. This is Yūki silk; the gemlike craft is *sui generis*."

"That coat's texture is flat as a page. There's no depth to the weave, it's all sheen. Unthinking variation."

"Did you see that guy's suit? When was the last time you *saw* someone in serge blue? That's a mark of the petit-bourgeoisie."

"I've figured it out now: your *obi*, it's tied like a *rakugoka's*! Get on the table and tell us a tale!"

"Is this Ōshima pongee? There's a group of monks I see every day walking in Yamanote. You look like one of them."

Such was the nature of their chatter.

Huddled in a seat at the foot of the table was a grotesquely thin man in a tawdry kimono fashioned from unbleached yellow rags, his family crest splashed across the back in primitive script. The kimono was so outrageously tasteless that it became the target of a roast, led by a young professor with a ferocious mane of hair. Standing up amidst the crowd, he pointed at the thin man and decried: “Look at his kimono, as glamorous as ever!”

The professor, starkly thin himself, wore a baggy, ivory gown like that of a Dominican friar, even if he was, in fact, aping the French novelist Balzac, whom he idolized; but because he didn’t have his idol’s brawny body, he looked feebly sunk in the whorl of folds and sleeves. The thin man cackled wryly, then fell silent.

A second man leaped to his feet and flared his chest at the professor. “Speak for yourself!” he yelled. “You’re always dressed in that rag!”

The young defender’s kimono was spun from an ambiguous type of silk, either Meisen or Ōshima. But he, too, was far from pristine, and it seemed as though he hadn’t bathed for weeks. He had a fetid stench, and there was grime smeared on his collar.

The thin man, giving no defence of his own, just sat there, looking like an extraordinary coward.

At the head of the table, an immense man in a bold-striped suit burst out laughing. He was muscular and broad-shouldered. Grinning with beneficent authority, he raised his hands to tame the uproar and made a show of clearing his throat before chiding the thin man half- pityingly: "Why didn't you wear what you wore last time? Your taste is regressing. At least the parched yellow matches the pallor of your face ... Everyone, listen up; lest we forget, this man changed outfits once before, so he can do it again. Let's not pick on him, but encourage him to change into something less offensive."

People cheered, *"Hear! Hear!"* Others heckled and booed: "Don't baby the man, he's not welcome here. He'll blunder again!"

When no one was watching, the thin man, hunched over and scratching his head, pussyfooted from the restaurant and into the night, racing back to his two-storey cottage on the outskirts of the city. Spread throughout the upper and lower floors of his home was an eccentric panoply of costumes, each hanging to air on its own wall hook. He had the exact thing in mind to wear: it was shiny, like the scales of a serpent. After digging around, he unveiled a partial suit of chainmail armour – jacket, boots, and gloves. He disrobed, and when he put on the armour, he felt his courage restored. He sat cross-legged on the ground and began smoking cigarettes, and between puffs he spoke at last ...

But it was then that I awoke.

And now that I'm awake, I can't remember what he said. This is regrettable, especially since I'm writing this story about the dream.

*Undated*

# EASTERN AUTUMN

I was walking through Hibiya Park under a shroud of mist. The sky was shingled with clouds; a blue fringe sat on the horizon above the trees. It was almost evening. The path through the forest was coated in dew – the sand, stones, and wilted grass, even the tangles of plane tree branches, the shadows of their yellow leaves blurring with the first twilight gleaming in the dew. I was the only person on the path. I maintained a brisk pace with my cane tucked under my arm, cigar butt between my lips. The branches crisscrossing above me rained down yellow leaves. In the distance, I heard the echoes of a fountain burbling as if it had been there for centuries, while the din from the surrounding town erupted as though from blustery waters, softening to a lull on its way to the lonely canopy above me. In the heart of the forest was an old pond, where there were cranes whose cries sometimes muffled the tender sounds of the fountain.

I continued walking; but the further I went into the forest, the more weighted I felt with ennui and fatigue. In my restless life as a hack, I pass so much time alone waiting in vain for some twilight of inspiration to grace the sky of my imagination, and as I reflected on this state, the park descended further into the twilight of the world – and I was bathed in smells of dirt, moss, and fallen leaves, mingling together on the chilly breeze and pierced by the cloying funk of fruit and flowers rotting, hidden, in the trees. Lying in a puddle in the middle of the path was a pale rose stem. Untouched by dirt, it looked as if it had been picked in haste and quickly thrown away. If only I could lay myself down like this rose, I thought, and sleep forever in this bed of autumnal scents, drunk on lethargy ...

But then I was halted by a presence up ahead: the backs of two nearly identical men, bent at the hip with bamboo brooms, sweeping at the dazzling mat of yellow leaves. They had bird's-nest-style hairdos and wore frazzled ink-black robes, and their fingernails and toenails were long and pointy like the claws of wild beasts. Standing there riveted by this spectacular pair, I witnessed an amazing sight: crows shooting up from the trees, tracing a circle in the clouds and then diving perilously, jockeying dance-like for a spot on the shoulders and heads of these men dutifully sweeping the yellow leaves of autumn strewn across the sand.

I spun cautiously around so as not to be seen; chewing on my cigar butt, I retraced my steps, brimming no longer with ennui and fatigue but with a joy as gentle and buoyant as the twilight. All this time I had presumed these two figures of lore to be dead, which was my own short-sighted delusion: Kanzan and Jittoku are *alive*, having survived the vicissitudes of centuries to rake dead leaves on this day in the park. So long as they live, my nostalgia will likewise live for autumns past in Tokyo, my dreams of which have the power yet to refresh a jaded hack like me.

At the front gates, whistling an upbeat ditty with my cane tucked under my arm, I departed the magical realms of Hibiya Park, the yellow plane tree leaves fluttering in my wake.

Sighing, I muttered to myself: "Kanzan and Jittoku live ..."

*March 1920*

*Translator's note: Kanzan and Jittoku (also known as Hanshan and Shide), were figures from the eighth – ninth centuries, low-ranking Zen Buddhist monks at Guoqing Temple on Tiantai Mountain in China. In Buddhist lore, they are depicted as incarnations of the bodhisattvas Monju and Fugen, who represent the virtues of wisdom and compassion.*

# KANZAN AND JITTOKU

Last time I visited my mentor Natsume Sōseki, he was seated in his library with his arms thoughtfully folded. "It's been a while," I said. "Am I disturbing something?"

"Yes," he spoke sternly. "I was having a vision of Gokoku Temple. The sculptor Unkei was chiselling at two blocks of stone below the great triple gates. Taking shape in the stones were the fearsome Niō, the muscular guardians of the Buddha himself."

Unlike Sōseki, I was indifferent toward the art of Antiquity, feeling that it was irrelevant to our uniquely torrential age, so instead I steered our conversation toward Tolstoy and Dostoevsky, which did not, however, go as planned. Exasperated by Sōseki's stubbornness, I took my leave and went to Edogawa Station to catch the train.

It was crowded. I secured a strap at the back of the carriage and began to read the book I was carrying in the breast pocket of my jacket. It was a Russian novel in English translation about the revolution of 1917, replete with harrowing scenes of the

Bolsheviks' bravery: labourers lobbing dynamite at the Whites; women joining the fight; the daily life of a revolutionary, suffused with bleak uncertainty ... in all of Japanese literature, there are no words that convey these feelings. I admired the intensity of the prose. As I stood there, I underlined passage after passage with my coloured pencil.

After transferring trains in Iidabashi, I noticed two curious old men trudging down the sidewalk. They were wearing the same ragged kimonos, and their hair and beards were long and unkempt. Their carefree, simpering faces had a quirky cast that gave them the appearance of being from a bygone age, and yet there was something queerly familiar about them. I wondered if I hadn't met or seen them somewhere before. A man grabbed the strap next to mine. He looked like the proprietor of a curio shop or some such place. "Look!" he said. "It's Kanzan and Jittoku!"

And then I recognized the pair. It was as if they had stepped out of a Taiga painting, Kanzan with his scroll and Jittoku with his broom. But it was too absurd to believe. Even at a rare-art auction, one would never see the equivalent of Kanzan and Jittoku in the flesh walking through Iidabashi. I tugged on the sleeve of the man next to me and asked: "Is that really Kanzan and Jittoku?"

He said: "Of course! I ran into them the other day, too. Outside the Chamber of Commerce."

"How is that possible? Shouldn't they be dead?"

"Are you blind? They're alive as they've always been, the reincarnations of Samantabhadra and Mañjuśrī. Even their old friend Bukan the Admiral is alive. In Ginza you can see him riding his tiger through the streets, bellowing his poetry."

Five minutes later, as the train began to move, I tried returning to my book, but its descriptions of dynamite odours fell flat on the page. I was too intrigued by the figures of Kanzan and Jittoku passing from our window and receding from view. In the placid light of late autumn, I could see Jittoku's broom propped against his shoulder, poking above his bushy head and bobbing with his step. Clutching the strap above me, I slid the book into my jacket pocket and stared through the window at the ancient duo shrinking to the size of beans.

That night, at home, I had the impulse to write a letter to Sōseki about what I had seen in Iidabashi. By the time I took up my pen, my scepticism from the train had faded, and the once farcical idea of Kanzan and Jittoku wandering through modern-day Tokyo seemed plausible, if not undeniable.

*Undated*

# FROSTY NIGHT

Memory of a frosty night –

I'm sitting at my desk when the clock strikes midnight, time to sleep. Earlier I had decided to go to sleep at this hour no matter what I was doing. I shut my books and tidy my desk so I can start work again in the morning. "Tidy" is something of an exaggeration, as all I do is stack my papers and books into a pile and extinguish the coals in the brazier by pouring water from the iron kettle into the bisque and picking up the coals one by one with the tongs and plopping them into the water, where I watch them sizzle and blacken. I take pleasure in the sound of the coals hitting water, the sight of the flocculent steam, the dramatic transience of this ritual. Before settling in my bedroom next to my study, I make a stealthy trip downstairs to empty my bladder without waking my family and notice that the light is on in the room attached to the parlour. Who could be up at this hour? Creeping up to the open door, I see my sixty-eight-year-old aunt on the floor, stretching fine silk cotton into luminous strips.

"You're awake."

"I thought I'd finish this batch before turning in," she says. "Are you going to sleep already?"

A minute later, in the toilet, the light doesn't turn on. I urinate in the dark. Outside the window is an endless bamboo forest. On windy nights the rustling of the leaves makes me shiver, but tonight, because there is no wind, there is no sound – only stillness, everything sealed in silence by the cold.

*Frosty night, silk cotton strips. No waiting till morning to be stretched.*

*Undated*

# SWAMPS: I

On a rainy afternoon, at an art exhibition, I discovered a miniature oil painting in the corner of one of the rearmost galleries. To say that I 'discovered' it is not an understatement: the painting was shoddily framed and hung out of sight in the worst possible light, as if meant to be forgotten – or shunned. It was called *The Swamp*, and its style was as unfamiliar to me as the artist's name. Perhaps because the work was minute in size and the subject matter superficially clichéd, with its imagery of floods, thickening mud, wild foliage and the like, I saw no one stop in front of it, or even begin to appreciate what a remarkable achievement that it was. For one thing, the artist used no green on the plants; the common reeds, poplars and figs were a viscous yellow that was textured like wet wall plaster. At first, I couldn't decide if the painting faithfully represented the artist's perception, or if it caricatured it. I admired the nuances of line and shade, and became convinced that the painting could only have been done by someone with a visionary eye: it had frightening power, but one that revealed itself only by degrees. I was entranced by the foreground mud, the intricate yellows of the plants, feeling myself inside the scene, ankle-deep in the smooth, gluey mud, hearing the sounds of my treading feet. In this modestly sized oil, this unknown artist demonstrated a command of Nature on par with the canonical greats. Of all the paintings on display that rainy afternoon – some by the most celebrated masters of our time – none approached the eminence of *The Swamp*.

"You're his number-one fan," a voice announced with sarcastic intimacy, and a hand clapped my shoulder, shaking me from the sanctum of my thoughts. I turned toward the man and recognized him as the art critic for one of the papers; I had spoken with him on a few occasions, and had never cared for him. "What's so special about it?" the critic asked, pointing at the swamp with the tip of his manicured beard. He wore on his spry body a brown suit made to measure in a style that was ubiquitous at the time, and he conducted himself snobbishly, with the calculated grace of a man who believes in his infallibility.

I addressed him with extreme reluctance. "It's a masterpiece," I said.

"A masterpiece? It's interesting, I'll concede that." He discharged a laugh. I could see his belly punching the inside of his shirt. Some people glared at us, thinking that we were a pair, which magnified my antipathy. "It has a fascinating story," he continued, "as it's the only painting in the exhibition that's not by a member of the Academy. The artist used to come in all the time and pester the office about showing his work. No one took him seriously, of course, and then one day he stopped coming and everyone forgot about him until his family began showing up in his place with his paintings in tow, making the same request. And their persistence paid off. The Academy finally relented and accepted this one, whatever their motives, as long as the family didn't mind it hanging back here."

"Is the artist dead?"

"Dead when he was living."

"What do you mean?" I said, more interested now than miffed.

"He went mad. Haven't you heard?"

"He was mad when he did this painting?"

"Obviously, yes." The volume of his voice had spiked. "No sound mind paints colours this detached from reality. But we disagree. You say this painting is a 'masterpiece.' For me, that's most perplexing."

He chuckled pompously. He seemed to think that I was ashamed of not knowing the backstory of the work, and moreover, he tried to exploit my ignorance by imposing his viewpoint on me. But his words were to no effect. I was arrested with wonder again by the swamp, and my vision of the artist as a petulant man, tormented by anxieties and an exquisite eye for the light.

The critic rested his case, sharpening his air of self-belief: "The man went mad by attrition, from his inability to get the images from his head onto the canvas. Say what you like, but this is the nature of the work that you prize."

This critic's lame assessment was the artist's only recompense from the establishment for a work that had cost him his sanity. I peered further into the swamp, and had a feeling again of unsettling clarity, seeing there the turbid waters and skies, the common reeds, poplars and figs textured like pulpy yellow mud, as dynamic as Nature itself.

I looked at the critic and repeated myself: "It's a masterpiece."

*April 1919*

# SWAMPS: II

*Walking on the bank of the swamp –*

I don't know if it's night or day. I hear the wail of the blue herons, see the watery light of dusk leaking through the canopy, the shadows of the creeping vines, the swamp and its towers of reeds. No motion in the water or the floating duckweeds, no ripples from the fish.

I don't know if it's night or day. I have walked on this bank for days, my body drinking up the cold dawn light, the stink of bog and reed. The frogs in the branches of the vine-swathed trees croak in turn at the dim starglow.

*Walking on the bank of the swamp –*

The swamp and its towers of reeds. A world once existed among these reeds, and even now, I believe, this world exists. I hear its strange and lovely vestiges, songs on the air from *"L'invitation au voyage"*. Only, where are the nectary scents of the Sumatran forget-me-nots in the bog and reed?

I don't know if it's night or day. In search of this world, I have walked for days among the vine-swathed trees in a state of waking dream. Flourishing around me, the towers of reeds, bound by the boundless swamp, which I must enter to find the forget-me-nots.

As I wade in, I come upon the gnarled torso of an ancient weeping willow, looming above the reeds. From the tree I know I can dive into the swamp, into that strange and lovely world of dreams. I climb the trunk of the tree, and at the top I throw myself headfirst into the swamp. On my descent, I hear the chanting reeds, the murmuring waters, and the frogs gasping as I break through the duckweeds; my body sinks like a stone to the swamp floor, an infinity of green flames flashing and flitting around me.

I don't know if it's night or day.

Velvet mud entombs my body, immaculately blue waters eddy around me. There is no strange and lovely world. By whom was I deceived? Myself, or the swamp nymph singing *"L'invitation au voyage"*?

A slender green shoot grows from the dead man's lips, punctures the surface and continues skyward, blossoming into a glorious white waterlily above the reeds and reek of duckweeds.

*Was this the world I was looking for? –*

The musing corpse, its eternal gaze at the pearlescent waterlily.

*March 1920*

# COLLECTING BOOKS

By temperament, I'm not a collector. Besides the insects I kept in primary school, there's been no object for which I've had the collector's flair – not matchbooks or oil pots, posters or paintings, early or modern calligraphic scrolls. I admire people who collect things, yes, but I despise them equally, too. And book collectors are no exception.

As writing is my trade, I'm constantly in my study, surrounded by books; yet I emphatically do not consider myself a collector of them. I cannot be. A real collector's shelves are defined by coherence and a sense of mastery, whereas my shelves consist of lawless rows and heaps that collected of their own accord. But to say my library is defined by chaos would be disingenuous, because my books – at the very least – reflect my tastes and their evolution throughout the chapters of my life (and on the separate subject of whether or not a book's contents can divulge an author's deepest secrets, I can't deny that they do).

For a while, I had maintained a catalogue of my books ordered by month and year of purchase, with the ambition of writing a sequence of vignettes about my life as each book entered it. However, when I learned of an identical work in the West I abandoned the idea – luckily for everyone, especially me, as a collection of books forms a mirror of the owner's interior and does not lie. It troubles me that a stranger could deduce from my shelves my inmost insecurities (which is why commingling different personal libraries – as auctions sometimes do – is an injustice tantamount to altering a story one didn't write).

I repeat, I'm not a collector, for I possess none of the typical traits, being immune to the mood swings and finicky preciosities. I tranquilly breeze through bookshops, flip through catalogues and buy what grabs my fancy; my method goes no deeper, and I spend relatively little money on books.

But I'll concede my doubts here too, as to whether all of this is not just another tale of collecting books.

*July 1924*

## A CERTAIN SOCIALIST

A young man decided to become a socialist, and when his father – a low-ranking civil servant – heard the news, he threatened to disinherit him; but the young man was not convinced, except of his own righteousness, and by the fervour of the friends with whom he had formed an official socialist party, meetings of which he never missed. Late at night, under light of an oil lamp, he composed essays that appeared in the party's ten-page pamphlets, which he and his comrades distributed in the streets and discussed at their meetings. Of all these writings, there was one essay in which the young man allowed himself to feel a measure of pride, despite it being weak in the area of critical enquiry that the party revered above everything. It was called "In Memory of Liebknecht", and the prose, which he thought exemplary, abounded in poetic ardency.

To the dismay of his parents, the young man's studies began to suffer, and a slumping record of attendance prompted his school to intervene. Unwilling to renounce the party, the young man dropped out of school and found a job at a magazine publishing company, then moved out on his own. He also deepened his commitment to the party, playing a star role in all discussions and debates, maintaining a flawless record of attendance and a rigorous schedule of writing and reading. He asked himself, "Of what importance are family and career when an international socialist revolution is underway, with our party at the fore?"

Around this time, the young man – forsaken by his family – fell in love with a girl who was not a member of the party; yet they married and moved into a cottage where he soon felt, as never before, instead of discontent, a happy fulfilment in his life with his wife, dog and their garden of poplars. One morning, his wife announced that she was pregnant, and his world was overturned once more. He became, overnight, obsessed with money and the advancement of his career. He sacrificed going to party meetings and stayed loyal to the socialist cause in intellect only, assuring himself all the while that he was the same radical idealist as ever – a fact venomously disclaimed by the party, the junior members of which were quick to brand him a traitorous quitter. Indeed, the party ceased to have a place in his life.

It was only sometimes late at night through his reading, under the light of his electric lamp, that he persevered in his socialist activities. On one of these occasions, he found himself flipping through the collection of pamphlets he had helped to author as a younger man. Reading his once prized piece "In Memory of Liebknecht", he felt that the writing was pathetically inadequate, and stowed the pamphlets away. The man had stopped caring about the party, and the party had likewise cooled to him, having deserted him in the name of revolution as he had deserted them in the name of family and career. In the years after their breakup, whenever the man ran into his old comrades, he would stop to chat; but not more than a minute would pass before he was confronted with their screeds about an "imminent breakthrough" in the movement, and he would nod along politely, contented with his staid life centred on career and family.

Decades later, after a near-lifetime of devotion to the magazine publishing company, having earning the full trust and respect of his seniors, he was promoted to an executive himself; he now lived in a mansion with his wife, with whom he had raised many children who were now adults and having children themselves.

But what about that other side of him? Did he still continue his socialist activities at night, under light of his electric lamp? God knows. Sometimes, however, lounging in the rattan chair on his porch and reflecting on his youth over an imported cigar, he felt those old pangs of disaffection, the only salve for which was the stoic resignation he had honed over the years – that classic fatalism of the East.

The now-old man was, in his mind, undoubtedly a failure. But little did he know that a prominent young socialist from Ōsaka with a burgeoning group of devotees had been inspired by the incendiary writings of his youth – specifically the essay "In Memory of Liebknecht". The young leader quoted from it in speeches and exhorted his followers to read it, elevating the writer's name from obscurity to the summits of socialist fame. The young man would tell the tale of his life: after losing his inheritance in a stock market crash, he happened upon an archive of mouldering pamphlets from which he unearthed the seminal essay, a momentous discovery that was the genesis of his conversion, of his unswerving dedication to the socialist cause.

And how little this young man knew, as well. Lounging in his rattan chair and smoking his imported cigar, in almighty ignorance of the legend around his name, the old man dismissed the whims of his youth with a single phrase:

"Human, all too human."

# RIVER FISH MARKET

One fair full-moon evening last spring, the gusty weather felt wintry to Yasukichi and his three friends – Rosai, the haiku poet; Fūchū, the Western-style landscape painter; and Jotan, the gold lacquerware maker – as they wandered toward Nihonbashi through the labyrinth of the fish market at 9.00 PM. I won't reveal the real names of the friends, but they were known in these parts for their achievements in the arts, with the eldest, Rosai, being the most acclaimed for his avant-garde poetry.

They had been drinking the night away – even Fūchū and Yasukichi, who were both lightweights; Jotan, too, an infamous boozer, had guzzled even more than usual – and they were holding their liquor admirably, all except for Rosai, who alone was in a precarious way, bobbling about in the middle of the group as they walked along the fish-smelling streets beneath the full moon. Incidentally, Rosai was the only one among them who could call himself an *Edokko*, a child of the city. His great-grandfather, born in Edo too, had been friends with Shokusan, Bunchō and many other famous artists and writers of the day, and people adored the fish shop, Marusei, which Rosai's parents ran out of their home. When the shop passed to him, Rosai hired outsiders to manage it so he could write poetry and practise calligraphy and seal-engraving in the Sanya slums. Because of this privileged, yet bohemian background, Rosai had a peerlessly bold personality, earthier than a Shitamachi bumpkin and a tad reminiscent of a Yamanote snob. He was, in short, as inimitable as the market's tuna sushi.

Rosai was telling his companions a ribald story, guffawing and gesturing so obnoxiously that his coat sleeves pranced up and flicked their chins. Jotan giggled and nodded along while the other two kept a step away. Upon reaching the edge of the fish market, the four shared a sudden sense of angst about ending their outing together. As they dallied into the open air, a shop curtain twinkling like a pearl in the moonlight caught their attention from across the street. It belonged to a Western restaurant known even to the reclusive Yasukichi.

"Should we go in?"

"Let's do another round!"

"Yes!" they agreed.

Mustering a second wind with Fūchū in the lead, they marched across the street and filed into the cramped establishment, where a fish market employee and a factory hand sat at a long, skinny table. The waitress seated the newcomers at the same table, two facing two, and they ordered razor clams and a bottle of Masamune sake. Yasukichi and Fūchū nursed a glass of sake each and gorged themselves instead on the clams and the other dishes they ordered. Despite its foreign name, the ambience of this Western restaurant was overtly Japanese; the table and benches were fashioned from unvarnished wood, and there were traditional reed screens separating the tables from the walls. Fūchū could not say if his steak was indeed a steak, or a charred grilled fish; Jotan wielded his knife with overdelicate clumsiness; Yasukichi was stupefied by the glossiness of the electric lamp, the first of its kind he had seen; and, as a so-called child of the city, Rosai acted like nothing was amiss, hunting cap pulled over his head in the style of Amida Buddha as he quaffed sake with Jotan and rekindled their chat from before.

Suddenly the front door flew open, and the curtains whipped about. A porcine man in a tiny fedora stepped inside, his grimacing face couched between the lapels of his fluffy overcoat. He stuffed himself between Jotan and the fish market employee, his flabby sides pressing against them both.

Yasukichi piled more curry onto his plate and thought, *How rude – in a Kyōka Izumi novel, the heroine geisha would cut him down with her wit and shoo him away. If only life were like that. Nihonbashi today is a different story.*

The man barked his order across the room, then lit a cigarette and began puffing smoke into everyone's face. Yasukichi frowned at the man, whose features now warped into those of a quintessential villain. His oily, flushed face and Ōshima silk jacket, his garish signet ring ... Yasukichi became so vexed that to keep his composure, he tried talking to Rosai on his left, who replied only tepidly, drawing the brim of his cap over his eyes and angling his back toward the lamp. Desperately, Yasukichi then engaged Fūchū and Jotan about the food, but these efforts failed too, for the fact remained that the appearance of the fat man had upset the mood of the room.

When the waitress served the man a bottle of Masamune sake and a platter of vegetables and fried fish, he grabbed the bottle and filled his cup, dribbling sake on his hands and the table.

Just when he was about to stuff himself, someone shouted, *"Kō!"* and he glanced up and nearly keeled over. As his consternation turned to shame, there appeared a radically different man from the lout who had just entered, speaking with exacting politeness and in a drastically higher key:

"If it isn't the boss! I didn't recognize you from here. I'm sorry!" He doffed his fedora and bowed at none other than Rosai, poet-proprietor of Marusei.

"It's been a while," Rosai said airily, raising his cup to drink, and after he finished, Kō reached across the table and neatly refilled it from his own bottle. Then, looking askew at his boss, he asked after his health and family ...

Yasukichi's fantasy had thus unfolded before his eyes. The spirit of Kyōka's novels was alive in the fish market district, where serendipity is still routine.

Later, when they were outside about to part ways, Yasukichi felt isolated from the bubbling company of his friends. He had no sympathy for the odious Kō, yet Rosai's negative appraisal of the man had brought no vindication. On the desk in his study was an open copy of La Rochefoucauld's *Maxims*. As Yasukichi trudged home under the full moon, quotes from the book played in his head.

*July 1922*

# OLD AGE

At the Gyokusenken teahouse in Hashiba, Tokyo, an *itchūbushi* school was hosting a practice recital. All morning, the sky was heavy with clouds, but by noon it began to snow. By the time night fell and the lamps came on, the ropes fencing the pines in the garden were sagging low with snow, which had piled up everywhere. In one of the teahouse rooms, insulated with two layers of sliding doors – one glass, the other paper – a brazier was shedding waves of orange heat, and the stodgy Admiral Nakazu, a brute of ill repute, had seized the inscrutable Rokkin by the sleeve of her smart, matte-grey coat spun of the same silk crêpe as her white kimono patterned with vertical brown twin-stripes.

"How about it?" he said. "You should take this off – it's warm in here, you'll dirty yourself before you play." Besides Rokkin, more than forty people were present: three aging geishas from Yanagibashi; the proprietress of a brothel in Daichi; the wives of the six or so retiree guests (including those of the Admiral and the gentleman fondly known as "Mr Ogawa"); the hunchback teacher Shigyō Uji and his seven or eight novice male pupils – three of whom, old enough to recall the Three Theatres' reign over the Edo *kabuki* and the Sannō Festival parades into Chiyoda Castle under the Shōgun's gaze – were locked in a double quarrel about a Gidayū recital at the Tobaya School in Fukagawa and a *senjafuda* collectors' gathering held at Tsutō's liquor shop in Yamashiro-gashi.

At twenty-four square metres, the crammed *tatami* room was the most spacious on the premises. An electric lamp, whirring in its bamboo caddy, pitched circular shadows across the cedarwood ceiling and the alcove, with its vintage copper vase containing plum blossoms and daffodils, slouched below the hanging scroll, the crown and foot of which were capped with yellowed strips of *Musa basjoo* cloth, the poet Taigi's verse enshrined in threadlike script on the stained paper: *Red fruits to the eye, birds and winter camellia.* Nearby stood a squat, smokeless celadon incense burner nestled in a rosewood stand, an emblem of the season's depths.

For the stage, two scarlet rugs had been unrolled before the alcove, their lively shades glinting off the catskin covers of the *shamisens*, the plectrum-wielding hands of the musicians and the stately paulownia bookcase, its side panels inlaid with *cloisonné* flower-shaped family crests. To the left of the alcove sat the women, and on the right side sat the men in order of rank, with Master Shigyō first, the Admiral second and Mr Ogawa third. Another one of the retirees, a contemporary of the Admiral and Mr Ogawa, occupied the lowest seat on the table's right side.

This unassuming man was named Fusa. He had celebrated his sixtieth birthday the year before last. His legendary teahouse habits had started back when he was fifteen, and by that accursed age of twenty-five he was ensnared in an abortive suicide pact with a courtesan from the Kinpei Daikoku House. In grief, he then frittered away the prosperous rice wholesaling company his parents had left to him, lapsing into poverty. He drank grossly, to cope, and roved through stint after low-paid stint teaching *utawaza* and freelancing as a *haikai* critic – until one day, a chance encounter with a distant blood relative ended in his salvation: his adoption by the owners of Gyokusenken, who gave him room, board and a pension. According to the Admiral, who knew him the longest, the young Fusa was famed for his mighty singing, which he would flaunt at night in the streets during the Kanda Festival, blazoned in a splashy *yukata* printed with droplets of rain on a path in a field, a protective amulet corded around his neck. These days, Fusa rarely sang the beloved songs of his youth; his once-supple voice had rusted over. He had even wearied of *kabuki*, having seen his last play in the year of the deaths of his age-old heroes, Ichikawa Danjūrō IX and Onoe Kikugorō V. Seeing the Fusa of today, in his bland yellow kimono, matching coat and brown Hakata waistband, attending sedately to the action onstage, one would hardly guess that he had spent his life in pursuit of artistic perfection and arrant debauchery.

The Admiral harried Fusa from down the table: "Fusa, what was the name of that girl of yours? The one from Itajinmichi."

"I know," Mr Ogawa teased. *"Okiku Yaeji."*

"That's the one! Tell us the story for old time's sake."

Fusa's diminutive figure shrivelled in his seat. "No, no," he demurred, stroking his bald head. "I can't tell it how I used to ... I'm too old. I have no feeling for it anymore at my age ..."

Nevertheless, to his own surprise, in movements two and three of her opening ballad, Rokkin's wistful voice and her *shamisen* strums, the lustrous major chords curling round the lovers' coos –

*Years on, the memory*

*of her ruffled black hair,*

*NIGHT FALLING stitched in gold*

*above the embroidery on your hem,*

*of Onatsu asleep with Seijūrō.*

– roused Fusa's timeworn soul, and he was enthralled, leaning forward at first then sitting erect. As Rokkin embarked on "The Peaks of Mount Asama", crooning the lines *Does love or regret, after sleep, cleave to the heart at morning?*, his eyes were clenched and adrift in a springtide vision, his bony shoulders rocking along to Rokkin's eminent *itchūbushi* cadence: the radiance, hidden in the rustic austerity, not heard in *nagauta* or *kiyomotobushi* schools, stirred bittersweet memories of his worldly life, now nearing its close.

After "The Peaks of Mount Asama", Rokkin sang "Flower Girl" as her finale, a sparkling duet that was met with an exuberant ovation. As she padded offstage, Fusa rose and greeted her with a reverential bow. "Please, take my seat," he said. "You must be exhausted." Then, at once, shattering the tenor of awe in the room, waitresses filed in with trays of food and drink, and talk resumed, along with the clinking of porcelain.

"Look at that, stiff as a cop in a box," said the Admiral, staring at Fusa shuffling out into the darkened corridor. "He's better off dead. I'd certainly rather be."

"Weren't you talking about him last time?" Rokkin asked.

The Admiral replied: "Ask *sensei*, he'll tell you about it. Fusa was a protégé of the Uji headmaster, too. And one of the best. He did everything brilliantly – *utawaza, itchūbushi*, even *shinnai nagashi*."

Mr Ogawa broke in: "And don't forget his collaborations with Murasaki from Komagata. She was before your time, but I'm sure you know the name. She and Fusa were preeminent. I remember their recitals like yesterday, and nothing today compares."

One by one, the seniors shared tales of Fusa's glories, and before long the three aging geishas from Yanagibashi ambled up to perform "Dōjō Temple", and everyone quieted down. Afterwards, Mr Ogawa was set to take the stage, for "Kagekiyo". He gingerly pushed himself up to his feet. His bladder ached, and he needed to gargle a beaten egg to crisp his voice. He excused himself into the corridor.

The Admiral seesawed up and tailed him out. "Ogawa, wait, where're you going? Let's have a drink out here. I can't sing if I'm sober, I get stage fright. I'm doing "The Potted Tree" after you, and I can't relax."

"We're in the same boat. I need an egg for my throat, but I could use a drink, too. A cup of cold sake. That'll prime the pipes."

They went outside and urinated in the latrine. Dawdling back through the long corridor attached to the main wing, they heard whispers. To their left were the glass sliding doors that led to the garden packed with snowed-on umbrella pine and bayberry trees, between the trunks of which yellow streetlamps with frosted-blue aureoles could be seen burning on the far bank of the river past the teahouse gates, where a plover couplet's shrieks went cleaving through the fog like sterling shears. At the moment, there was no singing, no *shamisen* being strummed; a great, glacial calm had gathered on the grounds of Gyokusenken, and the only sound audible to the men was the sea of snowy murmurs, tittering away like the needle of a sewing machine; snow falling on knolls of snow, secreting red spearflower drupes, skidding across green paper-plant lobes; and then, buried within, a whispering tryst ...

The two men had stopped. Mr Ogawa stifled a laugh. "If that isn't a cat drinking water, I wonder what it might be," he whispered bawdily.

To their right, fragmented voices slipped through the crack between the paper sliding doors:

*"Why are you sulking? Please, don't cry. There's nothing to confess ..."*

*"You're lying! You've been going around with that woman from Kinokuniya."*

*"What would I want with that old bag?"*

*"You tell me. We're finished. Go and be with your whore, see if I care."*

*"I'm sorry to hear that, but it's just not fair. How can you accuse me of cheating when you know that the only woman I need is you? Don't you remember my promise, back in the day, when we met at the utawaza rehearsal, after I performed "Possessions" – I remember that day like yesterday, how you ..."*

"Fusa, son of a bitch," said the Admiral.

"He's still playing the girls," Mr Ogawa said. He stooped forward and peered through the half-open paper sliding door. Both men, sporting lascivious grins, fancied they scented a woman's face powder in the air.

Inside, an electric lamp emitted an umbral, muted glow. A three-foot wide alcove housed a solitary hanging scroll from

Daitoku Temple and a cream-coloured Cochin vase with a paltry sprig of freshly budded Chinese daffodils. Facing the alcove, Fusa, in silhouette, bundled in a Hachijō futon coat with black velvet lapels, was seated on the floor with his legs heating in the *kotatsu*.

There was no woman with him. A quilt with navy blue and light brown lattice print was draped over the *kotatsu*, atop which two or three love-songbooks were laid open, and a small white cat with a bell collar sat posed in the shape of an incense box, its legs tucked in unseen. Each time the cat adjusted its posture, it produced a very fine, near-silent tinkling. Stroking his own bald head as if it were the cat's soft fur, Fusa continued to woo his fanciful lover.

"*... You told me I was magnificent onstage, and you were moved to tears by my performance, and my accomplishments ...*"

The Admiral and Mr Ogawa exchanged glances, then tiptoed down the long corridor back to the *tatami* room.

Outside, the snowfall showed no signs of slowing.

*April 1914*

# DIALOGUE WITH HIROSHI

"I'll become a rat and run away."

"Not if I become a cat and catch you first!"

"If you become a cat, I'll become a bear."

"And if you become a bear, I'll become a tiger and hunt you down."

"A tiger? If you become a tiger, I'll become a lion."

"Then I'll become a dragon. Dragons eat lions."

"A dragon?" Stumped, the boy thinks for a moment, then says: "Well, I'll become the storm god Susanoo, and wipe out the whole Earth!"

# A MORAL POINT

Have you heard the story about humans eating humans? No, not about the Russian famine. This one happened long ago, in Japan. An old woman was eaten by an old man.

And why did the old man eat her?

It was all part of a plot, concocted by an evil, old *tanuki*. First, the *tanuki* killed the woman, and then assumed her form. When her husband came home that night, the woman greeted him with a plate of meat that she described as "the finest *tanuki* meat". The man devoured the entire meal, not in the least suspicious of what he ate.

I'm sure you've heard this one before.

Yes. That's it, "Kachikachi Mountain". It's an old fairy tale.

Wait. You're laughing. Don't you see that this is a terrifying story? An unsuspecting husband feasting on his wife by deceit of a tiny beast. I can't think of anything more terrifying than this.

And, more than terrifying, the story has a subtle moral point: that we humans will gladly eat the flesh of our own, so long as we're blind to what we eat. Inside us all, the story goes, there lives a ravenous beast.

Now, returning to the tale of our *tanuki*, I'm happy to say that it ends on a satisfying note, with the *tanuki* perishing at the hands of a hare. Consider this death scene closely: the *tanuki* on its mud boat, ferrying firewood. The firewood goes up in flames. The *tanuki* and its mud boat sink into the river.

This is the hare killing the *tanuki*. And to think, a *hare*: yet another tiny beast. I can't think of a more profound story than this. But every time I ponder it, it puts me in a grim mood, for it shows the foundation upon which man's prosperity is built: *beasts killing other beasts*. A story that would make Zarathustra proud.

You're still laughing. Well, go ahead and laugh ... laugh. You have the ears of a *tanuki*.

*December 1922*

*Translator's note:* tanuki *is usually rendered in English as "raccoon dog", a raccoon-like canid native to Japan.* Tanukis *have a substantial presence in Japanese folklore.*

# KACHIKACHI MOUNTAIN

In the soft light of fairy tales, beneath the flowerless cherry blossom tree, the old man and the hare were mourning the death of the old man's wife at the hands of the *tanuki*. They were listening to the tongue-cut sparrows flap their wings and the distant echoes of the waves barrelling unbroken across the sea, as in the old man's dreams of sailing to Ogre Island.

The old man's wife was buried beneath the flowerless cherry blossom tree, its bronze branches cast like a net across the sky, where the translucent light of dawn hovered above the slumbering earth like a mist.

Without disturbing the old man's grieving, the hare rose up and pointed at the two ships anchored to the beach, one white and the other black, as though smeared with ink. Lifting his tear-streaked face, the old man nodded at the hare sympathetically, and in that soft light of fairy tales, they said farewell to each other below the cherry blossom tree. The hare hopped down to the shore, pausing to look back at its friend, who had hunkered down and was weeping again. The translucent light of dawn had filled the sky, where the tongue-cut sparrows now flapped their wings in the first flight of day.

Meanwhile, aboard the black ship was the *tanuki*, deep in thought, listening to the peaceful sounds of the waves and plotting to steal oil again from the lamps in the Dragon Palace undersea. If not that, it was rapt with envy at the amorous existence of the red rockfish.

When the hare reached the ships where the *tanuki* lay in wait, the tale of the two beasts began once again – from the rivers stilled by quicksand and the mountains afire, to the battles to the death at sea. In the soft light of fairy tales, the hare on the white ship and the *tanuki* on the black one rowed out to sea, as in the old man's dreams, as symbols of good and evil, the lullaby of the rolling waves girdling the two warring ships.

Lifting his head, the old man, still hunkered under the flowerless cherry blossom tree, gazed out at the shining white-combed sea, the grey clouds tensing above the beasts locked in their final confrontation. And then ...

The black ship is on fire and sinking ... *(Isn't this the* tanuki*?)*

As the white ship floats unscathed ... *(Isn't this the hare?)*

And the old man jumps to his feet, with light in his teary eyes. He waves his arms, cheering the hare's victory.

And look now at the cherry blossom tree, how it blooms anew with seashell shapes, as the pale golden sun swims through the translucent, light-filled sky.

This is the dawn of the fairy tale: man's delight in battles to the death between beast and beast, beneath the sun, with the cherry blossoms fixed to their branches like damascene.

# *SENNIN*

Once there was a *sennin* who worked as a jurist in O Town, near Lake Biwa. His favourite pastime was collecting gourds. He kept his vast collection inside a giant closet on the upper floor of his rented home, hanging from nails in the posts and lintels.

Three years had passed, when one day the *sennin* received a notice of transfer from the government. He was to relocate to a new post in H City. He made arrangements for all his furniture and belongings to be moved, except for the gourds, of which he had now amassed more than two hundred. He had no idea how to transport them, yet he refused to part with any of them.

*The trains won't do, and a carriage won't do either,"* he thought. *"The gourds are sure to break.*

After weighing his options, the *sennin* decided to rope the gourds into a boat that he could float across the lake, using for its keel a bunch of roots he had stolen from the Wandering Willow. On the day of his departure, as fortune would have it, the weather was clear and windless. The *sennin* boarded his boat of gourds and pushed himself across the lake with his wooden pole.

It's long been known that the *sennin* race had discovered the secret to eternal life in ancient times, after which they ceased to know death. And so, the *sennin* with the gourds was a truly unique specimen, for he was like an ordinary man, aging and – in his case – succumbing to stomach cancer. On the eve of his death, he raised his withered arms toward the ceiling and cried out: "Tomorrow will be my lucky day. Let's prepare to celebrate!"

The next day, rather than being a celebratory occasion for his family, it became apparent that the *sennin* had left a will more convoluted than any ordinary man could fathom. Understandably, his family did not honour it, despite the *sennin* leaving behind more than enough disciples who were ready to paint his gourds in the *nanga* style as his will prescribed. By the first anniversary of the *sennin's* death, his more than two hundred cherished gourds had been dispersed throughout the land, with no record of where they had gone.

*Translator's note: The* sennin *is a figure in Japanese mythology, variously translated as "wizard", "sage", "genie", "mage", "hermit".* Sennin *is a loanword from Middle Chinese.*

## *SENJO*

Once upon a time in China, there was a student who lived alone in the countryside. He studied all day at his window desk for the Imperial examinations, contemplating in moments of rest the peach blossom tree in the middle of the yard, as all people did in those days. Sometimes, in the neighbouring house, he would catch sight of a beautiful girl doing chores and find himself wondering who she was. She seemed to live alone and no one in town knew anything about her or her family and their means.

One spring day at sunset, after a long day of reading, the student stepped out onto the porch and heard, through the chirping of the garden birds, the girl shouting next door. Excited by this opportunity to meet her, he sprinted out the gates and up the path to her house, where he discovered a tiny girl with her eyebrows spiked in fury, shoving a burly lumberjack onto a bench and bopping his head with her fist. Although he was twice her size, the grizzled man sat before the girl meekly snivelling as if she were a giantess. The student, astonished, ran up and seized the girl's wrist.

"Why are you hitting him? You should be ashamed of yourself! He's just an old man!"

"What, *old*? This nincompoop's a kid. He's younger than me."

"You're a liar."

"Am not – I'm his mother, don't you see?"

The student went pale. He let go of the girl's wrist and examined her face. She was as beautiful up close as she was from afar, but he noticed now an anomalous grainy ruddiness in her complexion, and that she never blinked.

"Yes," she snapped, "this boy of mine's worthless, an embarrassment. All he does is make trouble. He doesn't listen and he's selfish, when he should know better – even at his age."

"How old is he?" the student asked. "He must be in his seventies. But if he's your son, how old are you?"

"I'm three thousand six hundred years old," the girl said.

The student realized then that his neighbour was not a human but a *senjo*, and in that moment she revealed her divine form to him and vanished, leaving her lumberjack son alone in the crystal light of spring.

*Translator's note: A* senjo *is a female* sennin.

# BIRTHING HUT

One autumn, a man was cutting reeds from the riverside to make into a birthing hut for his pregnant wife. When he finished the hut, he left his wife inside it, returned to the river and knelt in the reeds, praying to the goddess Amaterasu for the safety of his wife and child. At sunset, his wife appeared before him and said: "Come back in seven days, and I will show you the child."

The man wanted to see his child that instant, but he acceded to his wife's request. Night fell, and he untied his canoe from the reeds and rowed sombrely back to his village. The thought of waiting seven days was unbearable. He had a necklace made of seven crescent jewels, and each day, for solace, after watching the sun rise in the east and set in the west, he removed a jewel and set it aside. But on the sixth day, he could not wait any longer. That night, he rowed his canoe upriver, tied it to the reeds and sneaked toward the hut; it was so quiet and still that it seemed lifeless, save for the lush scents wafting from the reed-thatched roof. Softly, without entering, the man opened the door into the darkness. On the bed of reeds across the room he heard a measured rasping that he thought was his child. Eagerly, he poked his head inside and looked around. His wife was not there, and as softly as ever, the man entered the hut and crept to the bed. There he let out a scream, which shook the reeds all the way back to the village...

His reaction was understandable: his wife had given birth to seven albino rat snakes.

The shock the father had upon seeing the snakes is the feeling I have upon reading my own writing.

*Undated*

# MASKS

During my days at the University of Tokyo, I often socialized with a group of writers who were known for their contributions to the third and fourth editions of the literary magazine *Shinshichō*. It was because of their bad influence that I ended up becoming a writer, against my wishes. Admittedly, I'm overstating the point: I was also under the spell of a literary group from Waseda University, and if they didn't turn me into a writer, they certainly corrupted my penchant for healthy living.

The Waseda group consisted of Kōnosuke Hinatsu, Yaso Saijō and Tari Moriguchi, and together they had founded and edited a magazine called *Masks*. More than once, the poet Makoto Sangū and I visited Saijō in his dormitory near the Waseda campus. Saijō's room was illuminated by a lamp with a red conical shade, and it was here that I was introduced to the formidable Professor Kogan Yoshie, as well as Hinatsu and Moriguchi. I don't remember what we talked about, only that someone told a ghost story that was so effective that on my way home, hours later, I raced in fear through the drizzly night down the deserted streets of Ōkubo.

After that gathering, I lost touch with the group – first with Professor Yoshie, then with Saijō, Moriguchi and, finally, Hinatsu.

Some years later, while I was living in the Ōmachi neighbourhood of Kamakura, I ran into Hinatsu, who had relocated to Hase, near Ōmachi, and we started visiting each other again. The townhouse he was renting had a central parlour with an alcove that whistled fiercely whenever the wind blew, even with the doors closed around us. Hinatsu eventually moved away from Hase, and we've been out of touch ever since.

All the people I have mentioned are alive and well. Occasionally, I read one of Hinatsu's long-winded poetry critiques in *Chūōkōron*. But from what I gather, these days he writes in a room that doesn't whistle.

*May 1924*

# AS FOOD

In Kanazawa, people speak a language of cannibals. They use the word "delicious" to describe someone who's overweight. When they see such a person, they remark on the person's "deliciousness".

Every time I hear the expression, I find myself categorizing my friends by food type and method of preparation. Ton Satomi, I would slice like sashimi but leave unskinned. Kan Kikuchi and that nose of his, I would boil in grease and garnish with shiitake mushrooms. Jun'ichirō Tanizaki, that precious delicacy, I would simmer in European wine. Hakushū Kitahara, no doubt, would be delicious as a steak, and I have written before that Kōji Uno is a hunk of roast beef and Mosaku Sasaki should be chopped, skewered and grilled with no seasoning.

As for Murō Saisei (and I feel guilty writing this, as he sits across from me), I would carve him into strips and dry him in the sun. Not that Murō would mind. He might even prize the chance to eat dried strips of himself.

*April 1927*

# HARDSHIP

One spring afternoon, I had a meeting with my old friend Chito Tazaki at the publishing house where he was employed. I was seated on a chair in the narrow reception room. After some time, Chito appeared in the doorway, looking tired and distracted. I stood and greeted him with a bow.

"What brings you in today?" he said. He had a fountain pen tucked behind his ear. He was wearing a tattered suit.

"I have a favour to ask. I was thinking of taking a trip to Shuzenji or Yugawara to finish my book, perhaps visit a hot spring or two. I'd be gone for two or three days at most. I haven't been feeling well recently." The publishing house was scheduled to release a collection of my stories, and the purpose of my visit was to request an advance on my royalties.

"I suppose we can make arrangements," he said. "But those hot springs are pricey, from what I hear. I've never been, myself." Chito lit an Asahi cigarette. A look of childish jealousy clouded his face.

I said, "Why not? You're single. Can't you go where you like when you're free?"

"Well, as they say," he said, "no leisure for the poor."

I laughed, self-conscious of my Yūki silk kimono. "But you've been working here forever. What do they have you doing these days?"

Chito tapped the ash from his cigarette. "Editing and compiling travel guides," he said, and then his face brightened for the first time. "We're assembling a multi-volume reference on the subject, the first of its kind to date!"

*Undated*

# STRONG GIFTED MAN, WEAK GIFTED MAN

Sasaki is a strong man, and Kojima is a weak man; but both are gifted. I was out for a walk with Sasaki when he collided with a stranger and inflicted a rebuke that reduced the man to a baby. I was daunted by the might that he channelled in that instant. It was enough for me to recognize that he was not a common man, but a descendant perhaps of the Mongolian *khans*. Though Kojima, being a child of Edo, has a razor wit, I cannot imagine him confronting a stranger like this, and yet, both men are bookish in the extreme: when Sasaki visited me two or three days ago, he edified me on the topic of Luigi Pirandello's plays and the memoirs of Sarah Bernhardt; and Kojima reads with prodigious range too, as shown by his facility with the literatures of China, Japan and the West. (Despite what some noted critics of his work have said, his erudition is best showcased in his fairy tales, not in his novels.) Lastly, both men have the sort of good health that augurs longevity (poignant for I who write this from a sickbed). In their dotage, I picture Sasaki cultivating a shaggy beard, Kojima losing his teeth and both grumbling repetitively about "the ways of youth". No matter how low my life sinks, whenever I think of these men I feel my heart grow light.

*Undated*

# THE WOMEN I LIKE IN ROMANCE NOVELS

1. Either the purely good, or the purely evil – not one more than the other.

2. They do not exist in this world.

*Undated*

*Translator's Note: The author responds here to a survey in* Fujin Gahō *(*Illustrated Women's Gazette*), no. 170, 1 April 1920. The prompts were:*

> *"1. The women I like in romance novels are ..."*
>
> *"2. The reason I like them is ..."*

# SENTENCES AND WORDS

*Sentences*

I have friends who say, "Your sentences are too elaborate. Why do you write such elaborate sentences?" But I don't think my sentences are elaborate in the sense that they imply, for I aspire to brevity. Writing sentences faithful to my mind's eye, no more and no less, is my principal aim. It's easy in theory, but it scarcely happens without me muddling something. The challenge of sentence craft, the labour of it (if it can be called this), is in attaining the precision of a stone. I hold every writer to this standard. I disapprove of needlessly florid prose – I'm an Apollonian through and through. In defiance of my accusers' words, I grind my lines into calcite spears, and admit no ambiguity into them.

*Words*

Fifty years ago, a Japanese person hearing the word *god* would imagine a unisex figure with a necklace of crescent jewels and a hair bun over each ear. Today, the word *god* evokes another image in the minds of our youth: that of an aged Western man with a mammoth grey beard.

How fleeting our sense of a word is; it mutates as we speak.

*How I long to see / among the flowers at dawn / the face of a god. (Mount Katsuragi.)* One day, I was discussing this haiku by Bashō with my friend Komiya. Many years ago, the poet Masaoka Shiki interpreted the poem as a sophisticated exercise in puns, a knowingly playful piece. I've never disputed this reading, but when I brought it up with Komiya, he was adamant that the poem could only have come from an austerely spiritual mind, and was incensed that someone thought otherwise. Of course, neither of us was definitively wrong or right.

History says a painting can last for five centuries, and a book for eight. But what about a sentence? How many centuries can a sentence last?

*Undated*

## FLOWERS OF THE SAL TREE

Every botanical garden should have a sal tree. The only time I was fortunate enough to see one was in the garden of the house of a man whose name I can't recall; in the grass below the gem-like flowers was a complex, porous limestone called a Taihu stone, from Donting Mountain in Suzhou. What became of the stone's keeper is a mystery, except for the rumours I hear on the wind of him being around, living simply.

*It's the water month again;*
*Give voice to your grief.*
*Flowers on the branches*
*of the sal tree.*
*Eyes of the melancholy.*

*May 1925*

# GARDEN VERDURE

| | |
|---|---|
| *Cherry blossom* | Refreshed after rainfall. Petals below – still, calyx clouded pink. |
| *Chinquapin* | Almost time to drop the nuts the wee mice like to keep. |
| *Bamboo* | Even now, I have jaundice. |
| *Musa basjoo* | Oh, no – the wind cracked the chimneys on my green lamps. |
| *Plum* | By the time I shiver, it's already too late. The caterpillars are crawling on me. |
| *Fatsia* | It's so itchy, this light brown fuzz. |
| *Crape myrtle* | How can this be? So early. Look at me, I'm all dead wood. |
| *Kirishima azalea* | No teasing, please. I've been so busy this year; I bloomed these ugly pale purple things. |
| *Cactus* | Handle it however you like; it's not my business. |
| *Pomegranate* | Looks like my branches are caked with fleas. |

| | |
|---|---|
| *Moss* | Not awake yet? |
| *Stone* | No. Almost. |
| *Maple* | "Tawny youth of maple fades …" All downhill now. The artless pea-green of the young finches is upon us. Oh, my – how the lamplight flits across the paper sliding door. |

*Undated*

# ON A SUNNY SPRING DAY, WALKING IDLY ALONE

On a sunny spring day, walking idly alone along the street, I see the town roofer walking toward me. Nowadays, even he wears a blue suit and a felt hat with his rubber workboots. His boots are ridiculously big; going up past his knees, hiding half of each thigh, they look like something he stumbled into rather than put on.

At my friend's curio shop, a pair of items are on the redwood shelf in the front display: a Mushiake sake bottle with a vulgar mouth that reminds me of a Kobizen sake bottle that I once saw, the mouth of which was the spitting image of a girl's puckered lips; and a blue-and-white plate with the image of a man and his fishing pole beneath a budding weeping willow. Looking more closely at the man's face, I realize that it's the poet Murō Saisei, fishing in his hometown Kanazawa!

At the greengrocer's, only a few arrowhead tubers remain on the table, the courtly blue of their skin rivalled only by that of antique mud-cloisonné. I should buy some to surprise myself – now is the time, when I haven't meant to buy anything. But what does this mean anyhow, to surprise oneself?

The bird shop has birdcages of different sizes and shapes. In the middle of the shop is the biggest cage of them all, and inside it is the shop owner, reclining in his chair with varied tits perched on his body.

As I move along, two college students in uniform overtake me from behind. Snippets of their dialogue pass for the babble of madmen.

*In other words, it's the same as riding a horse.*

*But doesn't Kant mention him favourably in that essay?*

And then comes the hill. The slope begins, and up I go. The camellia tree at the house near the top is shedding flowers. The flowers on the ground are brown. Up ahead, a yellow bamboo grove crowns the hill, which ends with a cliff overlooking the sea. A horse gallops forth from somewhere beyond, tailed by white butterflies. Reflected in the globes of the horse's eyes are the stalks of bamboo, the camellia tree ... and my astounded face.

*These are fresh-laid eggs.*

*Oh, is that so? But I don't need eggs.*

On a sunny spring day, walking idly alone along the street.

*Undated*

# THE PARROT: NOTES ON THE GREAT EARTHQUAKE

*The following, as the reader shall see, are unedited notes. I have left them as is, as I did not have the time or the emotional means to do anything more. However, even in rough form, these words are not without value.*

*14 September 1923*

A *shamisen* teacher – residence in Honjo-Yokoamichō, Tokyo – his name is Daifu Kane – age sixty-three – lives with his seventeen-year-old granddaughter

House survives initial quake – neighbourhood erupts in flames – they escape to Ryōgoku – no belongings except their parrot in his cage – parrot's name is Gorō – Gorō's back is grey – his belly is pink – his only tricks are mimicking the sound of a jeweller's mallet striking metal, and shrieking "*I see!*" – which sounds instead like "*Icee!*"

Fleeing to Ningyōchō from Ryōgoku, he gets separated from his granddaughter – people in a frenzy – mountains of bags – no time to search – he sees a middle-aged lady with her caged canary – dressed like a brothel madam – "I see there's someone else like me" – time still for banter and grins

Arrives in Yoroibashi – half the neighbourhood ablaze – heat so intense he feels his face broiling – raining debris – lead pipes covering the electrical wires melt, fall – people duck and dodge, jostle against him and Gorō in his cage – cage stays intact – Gorō tirelessly raves *"Icee! Icee!"*

Arrives in Marunouchi – Imperial Theatre, Police HQ scorched – a titanic pillar of smoke above Hibiya blots out the sky – he sees the bronze statue of Kusunoki, goes to sit on the lawn, stands – paces – sits, stands – goes to shout his granddaughter's name in the crowd of evacuees – sunset – he lays in the shadow of a pine next to a stockbroker and his office staff – smoke curdles in the sky – everywhere he looks – crimson – Gorō in his cage, *"Icee! Icee!"*

Morning – resumes his search – Marunouchi first – then Hibiya – not Ryōgoku or Ningyōchō – "I don't want to return there" – noon – hunger – searing thirst – he drinks water from Hibiya Pond – granddaughter nowhere to be found – sunset – back to Marunouchi – he lies on the lawn, head propped on Gorō's cage so no one steals him – remembers the people at the pond catching ducks with their hands, eating them alive – he stares at the lights of the fire in the sky

Day Three – abandons search – journeys to Shinjuku to find his nephew – en route from Sakurada to Hanzōmon he hears Shinjuku is burning too – he reroutes to Yanaka – his family temple is there – he looks at Gorō and thinks of the ducks – "I can't kill Gorō," he tells himself, "but if he dies, I'll eat him to survive"

Next, Kudan-ue – government workers distributing raw rice – he takes his scoop, eats it uncooked – Gorō watches from his cage – "*Icee! Icee!*" – worrying that the squawks will be a nuisance at the temple he feeds Gorō the last of the rice – frees him on the banks of the canal – sunset – arrives in Yanaka – the temple is there – priest welcomes him in

On the morning of the fifth day, Daifu knocked on my door with no news of his granddaughter's fate. He was so haggard that I didn't recognize the spirited teacher I've always known.

*Coda: Daifu's nephew's house in Shinjuku was spared from destruction. After their separation, his granddaughter found shelter there.*

*Translator's note: The Great Kantō Earthquake occurred on 1 September 1923.*

## ON APPLAUSE

*Homes of Famous Writers*

Only now, the family of Sōseki Natsume is talking about selling the Sōseki estate. Their reason: it's too big for upkeep. It's about time they figured this out. They could've solved this issue when Sōseki was alive. The family didn't need a mansion. Sōseki spent most of his time cooped up in the two rooms that made up his study. They could've downsized to a home half the size, and Sōseki wouldn't have noticed a thing.

*In Pursuit of a Hat*

I was passing through a crowded part of town when a gust of wind knocked the hat off my head. As I cast about for it, I became conscious of everyone gawking at me. By chance there was a second man, a dapper-looking gentleman, whose hat went soaring from the same gust of wind, but as soon as his hat flew from his head, he pursued it doggedly. He crashed into a cyclist, dodged a car and cut off a gang of labourers with their wagons, who brandished their fists at him. But in the end he was victorious, nabbing his hat from the air and popping it back onto his head.

Life doesn't happen so auspiciously for everyone. With the exception of certain geniuses in the fields of politics and business, there are few people who could fetch a hat from the wind with consummate ease as this gentleman did.

*A Lone Wonder*

A woman on the stoop of her rear tenement, the wife of a low-salary employee, engrossed as if in prayer in the latest popular novel about the life of a fictional count's wife. I see the tragedy in her cosy elation, which I also find rather quaint.

Kean *and* Masks and Monsters

I heard a group of people talking about two foreign movies, *Kean* and *Masks and Monsters*. *Kean* is based on a novel. The premise of the movie sounds comedic, though it is classified as a drama. Predictably, the men identified with the protagonist, Shakespearean actor Edmund Kean, and the women identified with the countess, the wife of Kean's antagonist. *Masks and Monsters* features a married couple in situations that most people can't relate to. I may be wrong, but who, for example, has ever been mauled by a tiger and lived to tell the tale? I tried picturing myself in the couple's shoes, but ended up feeling terribly silly and laughing at myself. A dog bite, I can relate to, but a tiger bite is a stretch.

*Movies*

Trying to read between the lines of a movie is a disheartening affair. There are no lines to read between. Despite how beautiful the actresses appear, they are as hollow and flat as can be.

*Movies II*

Every time I watch a movie, I leave the cinema with a vacant mind. As soon as the movie ends, I forget everything about it: plot, music, themes, even the faces of the actors. I'm no different for seeing it than I was before. With books, on the other hand, even the most insipid ones forever hound my memory. Perhaps if I could hear the actors, I would retain something more concrete. And this isn't even because I like listening to other people speak.

*Dogs*

I was listening to a story about a soldier in the Russo–Japanese War who was wounded on the battlefield. Passed over by the medics, he died overnight, not from his wounds but from the

Manchurian dogs that scoured the area nightly for food. They ate him, starting with his penis, and then moved on to his belly ...

And it was here that I stopped listening.

*An Exposition of Error*

Sokken Yasui's *An Exposition of Error* is an amusing read. His central thesis has to do with the so-called "pragmatism" of the Japanese having no equal, evidenced by the success of Japan's modernization, unmatched by any other nation in efficiency and bloodlessness.

*Punishment*

Day of execution. Rare to see a man walking to the gallows on his own. Usually the hangman transports the prisoner on his shoulders, sometimes with the help of an aide.

A number of states in America have been moving to abolish the death penalty, even for the most heinous crimes. I wonder if Japan will follow suit. For people in this country, the prospect of having to live beside a killer is repulsive. But there is a solution to this: lock these people up for life and toss away the key. Is this not retribution enough? Anything more is an extravagance.

*Punishment II*

Restricting someone for life from going where they please, when they please, is sufficiently torturous. In the meantime, one would be ill-advised to deprive such prisoners of a labour that suits them. If I were serving a life sentence I would ask for pens, paper and books to pass the time productively – for what would be the point in having me twine rope or, for that matter, having a ropemaker write stories?

*Punishment III*

This happened when I was a student. One day after class I descended the stairs and went outdoors, where it was pouring. When I realized that I had on my indoor slippers, I hurried back in to get my shoes. They were missing from my cubby. I searched everywhere, to no avail. The downpour grew heavier. I saw someone else's filthy shoes lying on the floor, and thought about taking them, if just to get home. Ultimately, I didn't become a thief that day, although if I had, it would have been strictly out of necessity.

*February 1926*

# MEMORIES FROM THE RED GATE

## I

I was twenty-six years old, and still technically a graduate student. I had been planning to withdraw for a while, but because I was living so far away from Tokyo I let the deadline lapse by a week or so before I delivered my letter of withdrawal. The clerk, citing university policy, refused to accept it without penalty. "There's a mandatory thirty-*yen* late fee," he said.

In 1916–17, thirty *yen* was no small sum. I did a calculation in my head and replied: "That leaves me no choice but to be expelled. I can't afford to pay that."

The clerk frowned. "I would advise against that, sir. You're better off paying. At most places of employment, an expulsion on record will disqualify you from employment outright."

And thus, I was expelled.

Upon hearing the news, some classmates of mine from the Department of Philosophy tried to console me by comparing me to the philosopher Friedrich Schelling. "You're like Schelling!"

they said. "Schelling was dismissed by the establishment. And look at him now, they all study him."

Even if this was so, and if Schelling and I shared this trait, I could not gauge whether or not Schelling, too, would have bucked at the thirty-*yen* fee.

## II

Our most illustrious professor of English literature was the late Dr Lawrence. I only ever spoke with him once. We were crossing paths on campus when he stopped to talk to me, rattling on in a sinuous English that I could not understand. I stood there as if lightning-struck, dazed by his gabbling face. When the professor caught on to my confusion he asked, in English: "You are Mr K., aren't you?"

I replied, in English: "No sir, I am A." Then the professor, too, fell into a daze. Bending forward to scan my face, he turned on his heel and strode away.

## III

I participated with the rest of the *Shinshichō* masthead in the last graduation ceremony ever attended by Emperor Taishō. Because none of us, including Masao Kume, had the appropriate summer attire, we opted to wear our winter uniforms instead, and set out charily to blend into the assembly of students before the Emperor.

## IV

I remember Professor Koeber's flannel shirts, and his lectures on Arthur Schopenhauer. Even now, I can hear him heralding Schopenhauer as "the Supreme Thinker".

## V

During my second year at university, I received a four-volume set of Ernst Moritz Arndt's poetry from the German ambassador Arthur Alexander Kaspar von Rex, in recognition of my achievements in German studies. In reality, the award had nothing to do with my German talents and everything to do with an encounter I had with my German professor at the Kitadoko Barbershop. I was in the chair about to have my hair cut when Professor Koeber walked in. Out of respect for his seniority, I relinquished my turn to him. I believe that it was this – my gesture of respect – that resulted in the award. Not long afterwards, I remember selling this Arndt set to Ikubundō for six *yen*, virtually unread, and now more than ten years later I'm still no more acquainted with Arndt's poetry than

I was back then, just as I don't know whether or not von Rex still has the same ruddy face in Heaven.

## VI

When I was a second- or third-year student, Yukio Yashiro, Masao Kume and I participated in a demonstration against the English Department for its unpopular teaching policies. We gathered in Hitotsubashi at Gakushi Kaikan, and though our numbers were small to begin with, over the course of our march a crowd rallied around us and our songs of triumph were soon booming through the streets. At the height of our protest, Kume, who was hollering with sensational ferocity, collapsed as if his heart had caved, and couldn't stand or walk another step. Yashiro and I lifted him onto our shoulders and carried him down a desolate road along the train tracks, which led us back to our Hongō dormitory.

*February 1927*

*Translator's notes:*

*The famous Akamon ("red gate") at the entrance to the University of Tokyo is an occasional metonym for the university itself.*

*Gakushi Kaikan is the alumni association hall for the National Seven (formerly "Imperial") universities.*

# YOKOSUKA SCENES

*Café*

I was eating a soft-boiled egg in the corner of a café when a man came in and absentmindedly sat at my table. Startled, I glared at him, but he pretended that I didn't exist. He was dressed in a brittle business suit that seemed to be made from raw seaweed.

*Rainbow*

I was in the back of the armoury that's always smudged with soot. In the cloudy sky there was a sliver of rainbow on the verge of disappearing. I tried getting up on my toes to catch its scent. But when I did, instead I caught a whiff of kerosene.

*Five-Minute Photograph*

One afternoon in late spring, I went to take a five-minute photograph with a young naval lieutenant I was friends with. As advertised, the photograph was developed in five minutes. Looking at it, we were confused: there was no image, only the roman numeral "VI".

*Dried Mud*

There was a girl walking in front of me. She was perhaps twelve or thirteen years old. Her bare feet were exposed below the hem of her sky-blue frock, and there was dried mud all over them. As I stared at the shapes in the mud, they morphed into the continent of North America, with its mountains, rivers and railways. I was entranced by the richness of detail and forgot where I was heading. When I looked up, the girl was gone and I was all alone. Sprawled around me was Yokosuka Naval Harbour, the tall, triangular waves crashing on the docks.

*Undated*

# IN THE CITY (OR TOKYO, 1916)

I

Not as lovely, eerie blue as match flames in the breeze.

II

*–In what way do you love the city?*

*–Like a woman with a labyrinthine history.*

III

In the park, withered grass, candied in snow.

IV

The solemn red-brick prison put me in mind of medieval times. In the absence of guards, I would not have been surprised to see Joan of Arc herself on her horse, blasting through the gates.

V

Words of a hostess: "I can't. Tonight I have the cutlery." (*Meaning*: her turn to wash and dry the forks and knives.)

## VI

Plane trees proliferating on the roadside, with the odd sawtooth oak and trident maple. Police patrol this area all day, unaware of the classical lineage of these tree names.

## VII

A young geisha walking in my direction stops five or six steps ahead of me and raises her hand in greeting. I stop, too, charmed but also confused. When I glance behind me, however, I see a second geisha standing there with her hand raised, waving at the first.

## VIII

Things that most depress me: khaki lacquered chimneys; rust on tracks that stalls the trains; caged monkeys in rooftop gardens.

## IX

I was passing through an alley at one in the morning. Two mud-splattered construction workers were fixing the gas pipes underground. A mountain of shovelled-up mud was blocking my way. Planted on its peak was a torch; its enormous flame flapped in the breeze. There was no way forward except over the mountain, and the torch made this impossible. As I was about to turn around, the blackened upper half of a body emerged from the pit. It belonged to the younger of the two workers; he moved the torch to the side, then climbed back into the pit. Thanking him under my breath, I felt, more than anything, pity for myself.

### X

Sumida River at midnight: no matter how one tries, one cannot surpass the words of the poet S. M. – " ... flowing, like bean jelly".

### XI

A child's voice: "Mr —, let's play!" Charting the rise and fall of its tones: "Mr —" (#"Mr", angled approximately 30° up and to the right); "let's play!" (#"play!" – also angled approximately 30° up and to the right).

When will these tones leave my ear?

### XII

The many ways in which a blaze resembles a temple festival.

### XIII

Winters in Tokyo, the colour of pickled vegetable stems – especially on the periphery.

## XIV

Good place to think something through: table in the corner of a café; good place to feel solitude: the middle of a congested pavement; good place to find peace and quiet: theatre lobby as the stage curtains are raised.

*February 1927*

# SPRING NIGHTS

## I

In Marunouchi, on an asphalt backstreet between concrete buildings, the air stank of salad. I searched around for the source. There were no trash bins, and the road was clean. Was it my imagination, or something else?

A defining night in spring.

## II

**U.:** "Are you afraid of the night?"

**Me:** "What's there to be afraid of?"

**U.:** "Everything. It's like chewing on a giant eraser."

U's words, the definition of nights in spring.

## III

A young girl from China was in front of me, about to board the train. The spring night shone splendidly through the electric lights that colour all seasons the same. As the girl stepped aboard, I noticed some dirt on her earlobe – more than some;

every crevice of her ear was blemished. I bit down on my cigarette in disappointment. Inside the train, the girl sat ahead of me. We began to move, and I continued looking at her ears, which were now, however, pleasant and endearing.

## IV

One spring night, I passed a horse-drawn carriage on the roadside. The horse was white and gangling. I was tempted to run my hand along its bony neck and spine.

## V

Another spring night. I was crossing through standstill traffic, when I suddenly remembered why I had gone out in the first place: to eat shark eggs.

## VI

Daydream about a night in spring: the windows of the Café Printemps opening onto an expansive meadow; plunked down in the meadow, a roasted bird hanging its head in penance.

## VII

Quote from a night in spring: "Yasu took a green shit everywhere."

## VIII

One night in March, after putting down my pen, I was relieved to discover that my nickel pocket watch was running thirty minutes fast. In the next room, the clock read 10.00. I set my watch on the table and diligently rewound its minute hand to zero. I picked up my pen. Time never strayed as far as it did then, in my watch. But when the clock struck 11.00 and I stilled my pen again, I checked my watch – and was aghast that it now read *midnight*. I wondered if the heat from my own hands hadn't caused its hands to spin in haste.

## IX

Someone in the chair is polishing their nails. Someone at the window is darning lace. Someone in the garden is picking flowers in fury. Someone behind the door is strangling their parrot. Someone in the back of the small restaurant is asleep beneath the chimney. Someone on the boat is raising the sail. Someone is wiping tracks of char from the fluffy white-bread loaves. Someone shrouded in gas vapours is shovelling mud into a pile. Someone – no, not just anyone, but a rotund, middle-aged gentleman with a copy of *A Manual for Poetic Diction and Composition* open before him – reciting his favourite poems, written in the manner of the Chinese, about nights in spring.

*February 5, 1927*

# NOTES ON DELIRIUM

## I

My stomach is a whale. A whale, they say, Columbus has seen. Sometimes it spouts saltwater for days on end. Those voices wailing – I'm sick of them.

## II

Sometimes, when I'm afflicted with fever, a fern forest sprouts on my tongue, in my cheeks and between my teeth.

## III

Am I the only one assailed by vivid memories of the great sago palms during bouts of diarrhoea?

## IV

When my stomach rumbles, it feels like I'm giving birth to baby sharks.

## V

When depression ails me, it feels like lice squirming in the folds of my brain.

*May 1926*

# TWENTY REMARKS ON CHINA

## I

*Hankou, Europe*

Stillness. A British ensign reflected in a puddle. *Oops!* Smashed by the wheel of a cart.

## II

*Hankou, China*

Walking along a gravel road glowing like a ruby in the setting sun, littered with shredded lottery tickets, *mahjong* tiles clattering away in open-air sheds, I see – appearing under the visor of my helmet – the spirit of Hankou summers: a basket, toting warmth and sunshine plums.

## III

*Yellow Crane Tower*

Red-brick buildings. Kantō Tower (teahouse), and the Tower of Revealed Truth (photography studio). Not much else for the eyes to see beyond these two. But there's also the red-brown Yangtze

River casting waves of glitter across the glazed tiles; and the Dàbié Mountains across the way, on the summit of which stand two to three trees; and – below – the small, white walled shrine to Emperor Yǔ.

Me: "Where's Parrot Island?"

Mr Utsunomiya: "Down there, on the left. But don't even bother with that dump, it's just used for lumber storage these days."

## IV

*Lute Platform*

On the rim of the moonlit lake, a petite geisha at the railings with her bangs undone; raising a pink fan aloft, she broods on the black and glistening clouded waters beyond the thinning reeds, the sacred lotuses parked on the shore.

## V

*Dòngtíng Lake*

Although Dòngtíng Lake is called a lake, it isn't always filled with water. The name means "Grotto Court", and outside of summer it transforms into a gigantic mud basin that has but a thread of water running through it. (*Illustration:* piercing the surface from beneath, rising three feet above, a decrepit black pine and its naked branches.)

## VI

*Chángshā*

A town in which people are executed in the streets; a town infected with malaria and typhus; a town of sundry water sounds; a town where the warmth of the sun clings to the night concrete; a town in which the chicken populace is a menace, crying my name without rest: "*Mr Akutagawa! Mr Akutagawa!*"

## VII

*School, Chángshā.*

I visited the First Tiānxīn Girls' Normal School and the primary school it operates. A young teacher with an uncannily cutting scowl showed us around campus. Because of the boycott against Japanese imports, the classrooms had no pencils or erasers or much of anything like our schools back home; the students, all dourly anti-Japanese, sat at shabby desks furnished with inkstones and brushes from another era, slogging through their algebra and geometry lessons. When I asked if I could see the dormitories, the young teacher's expression darkened, and he said, through my boy-interpreter: "I must refuse; it's a delicate situation at the moment. The other night, five or six soldiers forced their way into the dorms and raped some of the students."

## VIII

*Peking–Hankou Railway*

I'm lying in my sleeping car on the train. The door is locked, but I feel unsafe. I get up, push my suitcase against the door and lie back down, staring at it. *A suitcase, to keep a squad of rebels at bay.* I wonder, if the rebels were to sack the train, would I still have to leave a tip?

## IX

*Zhèngzhōu*

Two pigtails dangling from the grand willow on Main Street, clusters of bluebottle flies gilding them like glass beads. Where did the heads of the criminals go? Did they rot and fall, get eaten by the dogs?

## X

*Luòyáng*

At the Islamic inn, through the lattice windows fitted with old swastikas, glimpses of a lemon sky occluded with clouds of barley dust.

*A child, asleep, in a stupendous cloud of barley.*

## XI

*Lóngmén, Guangdong*

The grace of the T'ang women and men worshipping a Buddha statue atop a shiny black wall.

## XII

*Yellow River*

My accomplishments while crossing the Yellow River: two cups of tea, six jujubes, three Chénmèn cigarettes, two-and-a-half pages of Carlyle's *The French Revolution: A History*, and eleven dead flies!

## XIII

*Peking*

Enclosed for miles within an impenetrable forest of silk and pagoda trees, the multi-storey purple palace and its yellow-tiled roofs. Whose vision was it first, to erect a metropolis in the forest?

## XIV

*Zhèngyáng Gate*

**Me:** "Oh, you have airplanes too! You've Westernized more than I realized."

**Peking:** "Yes; but please, don't forget to visit Zhèngyáng Gate."

## XV

*Prison*

Excursion to the Second Capital Prison. One of the prisoners there, serving an indefinite sentence, builds toy rickshaws from scratch every day.

## XVI

*The Great Wall of China*

After a cursory survey of Jūyōng Pass and the limestone Zither Gorge, as we were resuming our climb of the Great Wall, we caught the attention of a street urchin. He began to stalk us, and before long he usurped the lead, pointing at the chain of wraithlike mountain peaks and yelling: "*Mongolia! Mongolia!*" – a geographical error we didn't need our maps to see. For spare change, the boy was attempting to exploit the Sino-Romanticism we held as learned Japanese, rooted in our study of Zēng Xiàn Zhí's *Eighteen Abbreviated Histories of Ancient China*. I was amused, moved even, to see such panache in a street urchin in this great and ancient nation in decline.

Nonetheless, at the sight of the edelweiss flowers in bloom on the ramparts, I had the feeling of being at an outpost, sequestered at the edge of the world.

## XVII

*Lóngmén Grottoes*

The transcendent flux of artistic energy – stone lotus gardens in the stone Buddha caves, petalled voices of stone gushing with praise. I hear the diapason of their songs, and am shaken by life's fragility.

"Please," I whisper, "let me breathe."

## XVIII

*Tientsin*

**Me:** "In a funny way, these Western-style towns make me homesick."

**Mr Nishimura:** "How many kids did you have again? Was it one or two?"

**Me:** "I'm sorry, I wasn't talking about Japan. I only meant that I want to return to Peking."

## XIX

*Shěnyáng*

Sunset at the train station, a band of forty to fifty Japanese people closing in on me. A terrific image, almost enough to make me cry "*Yellow Peril!*" and flee.

## XX

*South Manchuria Railway*

The centipede, scrabbling through the sorghum roots.

*Translator's note: In 1921, Akutagawa spent four months travelling through China as a journalist for the* Ōsaka Mainichi Shimbun.

# SELECTED NOTES FROM KUGENUMA

## I: Azumaya Inn

I was lying face up with my eyes closed. We were staying on the second floor of the Azumaya Inn in Kugenuma. My wife and aunt were sitting across from each other with my head on the pillow between them. They were gazing out at the ocean beyond the garden. When I said, "It's going to rain", they kept silent as if I were not even there. Finally, my wife replied: "Not with the weather like this." Not more than two minutes later, an unusually robust downpour came crashing down.

*

I was walking along a street lined with pine trees. There was no one else around. Only a stray white dog was walking ahead of me, swaying his rear suggestively. I could see his testicles, taut and pale rouge from the cold. When he reached the intersection, he turned around and beamed at me maniacally.

*

A tree frog squirming in a roadside sandpit, struggling to get free. The first thought I had was, *what would happen to it if an automobile drove by?* Granted, the road was so narrow that the odds of this happening were nil. But say that it did, would the tree frog be squished, or would it live? I began feeling pessimistic about its prospects, and decided to chip it to safety with my walking stick. I watched the tree frog land in a thicket of grass and hop away.

*

A Western-style house among the pine trees: the trees bending in the wind, the house bending with the trees. I thought my eyes were playing tricks on me, but no matter how many times I blinked, the house continued to bend in lockstep with the trees – a ghastly mirage.

*

I went down to the public baths at eleven in the evening. A young man was by himself in the washing area, rubbing his face and body with his hands instead of the customary cloth. He was frightfully gaunt, and as sallow as a plucked hen. I was so disgusted by his manner and appearance that I left without bathing. Once I got back to my room, I found a bellyband coiled on the floor in the entryway. I undid the sash around my waist and patted my stomach. The bellyband on the floor was mine. It had been missing the entire time I was out.

### II: Rental Home

Even in my dreams, I always am who I am. Last night (19 July): riding in a horse-drawn carriage with my friend Mosaku Sasaki, we conversed with the straw-hatted coachman about the cost of living in Peking. Within twenty minutes of waking from this dream, I was paralyzed with gloom, trapped in the dark grey tent of my head with no escape, a tear in the fabric letting in sunrays. My destiny is to deteriorate one day at a time, beginning with my head.

*

Out walking, I ran into a group of children in white bathing suits. They had bamboo husks sticking up from behind their ears. They looked like monster hares. When I was five or six steps away from them, I grew terrified, as if they really *were* monster hares with razor-sharp ears. I rushed by, trying not to be seen. Even after they were behind me my fear of them stuck, and I continued to hurry without looking back.

*

Lazing around and smoking cigarettes, I was plagued by distasteful thoughts. In the next room, the maid was folding diapers. Her back faced me. Out of nowhere I yelled: "Watch out for the caterpillars in the diapers!" and she cried: "Oh, my, they're everywhere in here!"

*

The other day, I opened a tin of butter and had a memory from a summer in Karuizawa. I felt a tingling on the nape of my neck, and glanced behind me just in time to see a horse botfly swooping across my field of vision – an everyday insect in Karuizawa, but a rarity in Kugenuma, if not an impossibility. Those unmistakable emerald green eyes: I can't deny what I had seen.

*

Nothing more dreadful than the dismal, windy days of late, the feeling of the world tightening its grip around my neck. Even my fear of lightning and dogs doesn't compare to my fear of the wind. The day before yesterday (18 July), I managed to stroll by a pack of baying dogs without even flinching, while a moderate wind-swell in the pines was enough to send me bolting to my wife in the quilts at midday.

*

Walking alone in the neighbourhood, I discovered a house that had been converted into a dentist's office. A few days later, I was out with my wife when we came to the very spot where the dentist's had been, except now it was not there.

"It was here!" I said. "I'm sure of it."

"Well, clearly you're wrong," my wife said.

That evening, to settle our dispute, we consulted with her mother, who's an expert in the neighbourhood's history, and she, too, affirmed that there was never such a house, though I was certain that I had seen it. I remembered the distinct layout of the sign: the character for *tooth* in the original Chinese and *doctor* written in *katakana* script.

*20 July 1926 (published posthumously)*

*Translator's note: These vignettes were written during a recuperative sojourn in the coastal town of Kugenuma, Kanagawa Prefecture, the year before the author died of a barbital overdose.*

# TEN THORNS

## I

*People I*

Such people exist who seek to dissect every bit of the world, who rely on the logic of a botany text to feel the beauty of a rose. If only they knew: to dissect is to *destroy*.

Blessed are the intuitive among us, for the analytical lack sincerity, trapped in the terror of their never-ending game. They mutilate happiness and exalt anguish in the name of *analysis*.

*Had they never been born* ... are the words that I begrudge these men.

## II

*We*

We are not whom we think we are. Our ancestors, undying, live inside us, and to ignore them is to assure our misfortune. *Karma*: a metaphoric account of perpetual agony. "Self-discovery", in its fullest, extends beyond the scope of the "one" and encompasses our ancestors and the gods themselves, who have ruled us for all time.

## III

*The Raven and the Peacock*

The most horrifying truth for man is that he can never be more than man. Freed from the blinders of grandeur, one sees this incontrovertibly – that a raven, however hard it tries, will never be a peacock; and that one line of a poet's poetry is a summation of all his poems.

## IV

*Bouquets in the Firmament*

Science explains everything. In the future, science will continue to explain everything, and yet, we esteem it merely as we esteem art, as token bouquets to raise in our firmament of achievement. Even if we deny the sentiment *"l'homme c'est rien"*, what differentiates us from our fellow men? Visionary bands of Baudelaires populate the halls of our mental wards, but who among them has borne fruit such as *The Flowers of Evil* or *Small Prose Poems*?

## V

$2 + 2 = 4$

$2 + 2 = 4$ is inarguable fact, but the + sign, in actuality, contains a myriad of gradations, each subtler than the last. All problems, in this sense, are subsumed within the + sign.

## VI

*Heaven*

Even if one could construct Heaven, it would inevitably be a terrestrial place. Do we not imagine it to be this way – a place with roses flowering amidst thorns, men basking in despair disguised as complacency, and dogs trotting everywhere? Doubtless, there are far worse lots than ending up a dog.

## VII

*Penitence*

The heart of man thrives in penitential misery, the standard formulation of which is "I shall not do again what I *did*", or: "I shall do from now as I *say*."

## VIII

*People II*

Such people exist whose greed knows no limits, for whom the prospect of having only one woman or one idea or one China pink or one slice of bread is abhorrent, and who therefore live at the pinnacle of indulgence, which is also the pinnacle of despondency. They are slaves to their cravings, denying to the very end the suffering at the root of their demise.

Even if one served them enlightenment on a silver plate, or guided them to the base of Heaven's stairs, they would balk on the grounds that "enlightenment" and "Heaven" cannot be theirs to keep. Not even a custom peacock-feather fan or a sumptuous roasted suckling pig is enough to quell their appetites. No matter how much they acquire in life, or how much they achieve, they are faced with insoluble sorrows beyond the normal sorrows of man.

A slim trench separates the piggish from the temperate, and the former are exceptional idiots. The only way to save them is to change them into new people. Hence, they cannot be saved.

## IX

*Voice*

"It is assumed that one voice among many will never be heard. This is wrong – *so long as the flame burns in the human spirit.*"

As it happened, one just had to wait for the dawn of the microphone.

## X

*Words*

We cannot easily communicate our states of being. The act depends, crucially, on the state of our listener. The story of Gautama's silent transmission of the Flower Sermon to his pupil Mahākāśyapa is one of veritable wonder; even newspaper stories hundreds of lines long fail to impart any empathy for a stranger's feelings.

The one who understands a person's words as he does is, by definition, the person's 'second self'. But man grows like a plant over time, and, perhaps with the exception of such a self, no one will remain to comprehend him. Man is doomed to become a stranger to his own being. Only with luck will he have a 'second self' somewhere convinced of his grasp of the 'first'.

*July 1927 (published posthumously)*

# RECORD OF EYES AND EARS

*Character, strangely enough, reveals itself in the lines of the neck. Dull lines portend, among other things, a hard head or insensitivity.*

*And voices reveal no less. Terse speech: a badge of strength.*

*Bamboo, seaweed, buckwheat noodles. What's more fantastical than a cat that dines on human delicacies?*

*Portrait of a religious fiend: his stellar skin; stung by zeal in conversation, he squeezes one eye shut as though aiming a gun, and fires his thoughts at everyone.*

*I was talking with a girl whose left eyebrow crinkled whenever I became excited about what I was saying. I wonder if there are many eyebrows like hers in the world.*

*I showed pictures of women to a group of men I knew to be of like disposition and education, and had them choose whom they thought was the prettiest. Of the twenty-five men I asked, only two chose the same woman, which means that a margin of no more than four percent decided the consensus pick. For what it's worth, as I pointed out, the subjects were all men, and of like disposition and education.*

*From my conversation with the fruit stand girl: "Honestly, in the beginning I thought I was staring at a watermelon floating in the river, not the head of a drowned man."*

*I don't know why, but when I see the hands of overweight people, I think of the fins of earless seals.*

*I can recall three instances of trophies in the lives of women. One: a mother suckling her second-born (boy) with her back to her firstborn (girl). Two: a collection of school medals on the breast of a waitress. Three: the baby a man's wife, a one-time hostess, cradles in front of their guests.*

*April 1927*

# NAGASAKI

*Climbing through the sky over the sacred mountain. Kites gliding together on high.*

*At the roadside fruit stand, bitter summer oranges and bananas. Sparrows swarm about town, the mark of a sunburnt pavement.*

*In Maruyama, the pleasure district, I pause to reflect on a willow tree.*

*Stone arch bridge that spans the canal. Procession of straw hats. Ducks swimming under the bridge reappear lit up like suns.*

*Lizard on the stone steps of Nankin Temple.*

*Flag of the Republic of China. A British vessel departs, huffing smoke.*

*"Newborn mountain leaves festoon the dock, like studs of light ..." – Mokichi Saitō, thinning hair on his blushing scalp. Pierre Loti. Shen Nanping. Kafū Nagai.*

*Last stop, Basilica of the Twenty-Six Holy Martyrs of Japan. Statue of Mother Mary in the chancel. Cornflowers mixed with ears of barley. Candlelight on a dark afternoon. Windows. Sky. Seclusion above the sacred mountain.*

*Diamond-shaped kite over the mountains. Kites from the songs of Hakushū Kitahara. Kites gliding together on high.*

*Undated*

# KARUIZAWA

*Landscape mirrored in the flank of a black mare.*

*Breakfast: toast with blooms of* rainbow pink.

*Flocks of angels crafting gramophone vinyl wings.*

*Outside town, ink runs over the roots of the chestnut tree.*

*Scrabbling up the green hill crust. Soap bars go tumbling.*

*Cucumbers bundled in the English weeklies.*

*Who smeared honey on the walls of the inn?*

*Madame M. – Butterfly dreams on the tongue.*

*Mr F. again, with his ratty bangs.*

*Mr O.'s moustache flutters like ostrich wings.*

*The poet S. M. – "Tips of the pampas grass stitch themselves into a pelt."*

*Face of the priest – then, his navel!*

*The slippery path that ends in napkins and lace.*

*Moon above Usui Pass: growing whitish moss.*

*Death of Madame H. – French phantoms in the fog.*

*Gadflies lumped all over Mercury.*

*Annoyance – hammock against my forehead.*

*Thunder is even spicier than pepper.*

*In the mountains, on a crag known as "The Giant's Seat", I see the unblinking face of a man climbing alone.*

*Everyone in that family has pink gums.*

*"Sheep steak garnished with fern leaves, please."*

*Goodbye, accordion town. Goodbye, lyric days.*

*Dated 1925*

# HACK WRITER: A PLAY

Characters:

**WRITER**
**EDITOR**
**MASKED MAN**

EDITOR: Can you contribute a story for next month's issue?

WRITER: It's not a good time for me. I've been sick, I haven't been writing.

EDITOR: But I'm asking you especially ...

*The two embark on an exchange so long that it could be a book in itself.*

WRITER: ... again, I'm sorry, but because of the circumstances, I have to refuse. I hope you understand.

EDITOR: This puts me in a bind. All I need is two or three pages. As long as it has your name, I'll take it.

WRITER: That's an insult to your readers. You'll ruin your reputation, peddling dog meat as sheep.

EDITOR: We have nothing to lose publishing a story by you. We only gamble on stories by unknown writers, because with these, whether they're good or bad, people hold us accountable. But if the writer is famous and the story is bad, people blame the writer, not the magazine.

WRITER: How do you know my reputation can afford the damage?

EDITOR: You're a big name. One or two flops won't affect you in the long run.

WRITER: By your logic, stealing five or ten yen from someone is ethical, so long as they're rich. I pity the one being robbed either way.

EDITOR: We're not talking about stealing, or about money. Why not see your contribution as a service to your readers?

WRITER: You must be joking; there's no such thing. A magazine buying a story from a writer is business, and when it turns around and sells that story to a reader, it's also business. Say what you like about editorial mission and standards of taste, profit is your primary concern ... literary merit is second, and everything else is a front. If a writer's work sells, you publish them, and if it doesn't, you don't; it's as simple as that. And besides, magazines don't care about the writer anyway, so why expect the writer to care about you? A writer should look after their own interests, not yours or anyone else's.

EDITOR: We have over a hundred thousand readers. What about them? Is their happiness not important?

WRITER: Only a child would fall for that argument. Even a middle-school kid sees a magazine for what it is, unsentimentally. It's not about pleasing readers, but selling issues to them, and what better lure than someone famous?

EDITOR: I'm speaking honestly. It's my duty to fulfil our readers' wishes.

WRITER: That's what you say. But you only give your readers what they want, because that's what sells.

EDITOR: I am sorry you feel this way, but it's not about profit, not for me. I'm asking you because I admire your work, as a reader – there's no calculation beyond this. I can ask any writer I want, but I'm asking you.

WRITER: Maybe your intentions are good, but I'm too soft of a person. People like me are easy to persuade. Even when I say I'm not writing, if someone asks me to write something I end up feeling obligated, even if it's impossible, and I make promises that I can't keep without my work suffering – this is not in my interest, nor is it in yours. If I'm not hurt by my own shoddy story, you surely will be.

EDITOR: If you're so sensitive to what people think, take heart from your readers and write something good – anything.

WRITER: Inspiration doesn't come ready-made.

EDITOR: You're overthinking it; all I'm asking for is something small – please, I can't leave empty-handed.

WRITER: Why won't you take no for an answer? What if I transcribe this conversation and give it to you? Would you publish it?

EDITOR: Yes, if that's all that you can manage. Just make sure I have the copy no later than the middle of this month.

*A Masked Man appears between them.*

MASKED MAN: *(To the Writer)* You worthless coward, one moment you defend a lofty ideal and the next you step all over it by colluding to write this hack piece. What about that reputation of yours that you cherish? One night, a long time ago, I witnessed Balzac himself write a novel in one sitting, stopping only to cool his feet in the tub. You count yourself among the living, but compared to Balzac you are dead! Stand your ground for once. I weary of watching you make the same mistakes.

*(To the Editor)* You too are a disgrace, publishing stories with no attention to quality. In America, magazines are sinking from lawsuits related to this very issue. Look past profit and circulation for once, and set higher standards for yourself!

*The Writer and the Editor stand there speechless, watching the Masked Man and waiting for his next move.*

*Dated 1921 (incomplete)*

# TIGER STORIES: A PLAY

Characters:

**FATHER**
**SON**
**MOTHER**

*An evening in December. Father and Son sit at a table, beneath which a brazier warms their legs. The Father hugs his Son. The Son is five years old.*

SON: Father, let's hear a story!

FATHER: What kind of story?

SON: Any kind of story. How about a story about tigers?

FATHER: Tigers? I don't know anything about tigers.

SON: Can't you make something up?

FATHER: I can try. *(He thinks)* A story about tigers ... Once upon a time in Korea, there was a soldier. He was a bugler, and one night he had too much to drink and fell asleep at his mountain post. As he lay there snoring, fast asleep, he felt something moist tickling his nose. His eyes fluttered open and he saw a sopping wet tail brushing across his face. It was a tiger.

SON: *(Incredulous)* Why didn't the tiger just eat him?

FATHER: He was about to, but the bugler smelled so badly of wine that the tiger needed to get rid of the stench.

SON: Then what did the bugler do?

FATHER: He grabbed his horn, and with all his might jammed it up the tiger's rear. The tiger yelped and fled down the path toward the town below.

SON: Did the tiger die?

FATHER: He was injured, gravely – the horn was lodged far up his rear. He left a trail of blood behind him as he limped into town. Each step he took the horn gave a toot, and in the middle of town square, in front of everyone, the tiger collapsed and died.

SON: *(Laughing)* What happened to the bugler?

FATHER: The bugler became a hero. The townspeople threw a celebration and cheered him for slaying the tiger, who had terrorized the town for many years. *(Pauses)* The End.

SON: *(Rolling his eyes)* That's it? Tell me another. A good one, something longer.

FATHER: But not about a tiger.

SON: Why not?

FATHER: Because. There's only so many stories you can tell about a tiger –

SON: *(Interrupting)* But what do you mean? Just make up one more, Father, please ...

FATHER: *(Sighing)* I really have to think ... Okay. Another tiger story. This one happened in Korea, too. Once upon a time, a hunter was hunting in the mountains when he saw a tiger prowling in the valley below.

SON: *(Wide-eyed)* How big was this tiger?

FATHER: Huge; the biggest he had ever seen. The hunter fancied it would become the crown trophy of his collection, and planned to mount the tiger's head on his wall. He loaded his rifle and took aim, but then –

SON: *(Interrupting)* Bam! The hunter shot the tiger dead!

FATHER: – as he was about to pull the trigger, the tiger, sensing danger, shrank down and tried to jump onto a boulder. It bungled the jump and tumbled to the ground, where it landed on its back with a thud.

SON: Did the hunter shoot it in the air?

FATHER: No, the tiger was such a blimp that it couldn't jump to save its life. It rolled over onto its paws, clomped back a few steps and tried again.

SON: And did it make it?

FATHER: *(Shaking his head)* No. it fell, then got up, wagging its tail in shame. After looking around, the tiger lumbered into the bushes, never to be seen again.

SON: So the hunter didn't even shoot?

FATHER: He couldn't bring himself to do it, not after seeing how clumsy the tiger was. He felt bad for it. The tiger reminded him of a human – the bumbling face, the laboured breathing. The hunter sighed and moved along ...

SON: Father, that's the dumbest story I've ever heard. Tell me a better one than that.

FATHER: How about a story about a cat? I know a good one about a cat who wears leather boots. Once –

SON: *(Interrupting)* But I want to hear a story about a *tiger*. I asked for a story about a tiger, not a cat.

FATHER: But there's more to this world than tigers, son. Tigers aren't the only animals in the world. *(Miffed, he thinks)* This is the last story; no more after this. Once upon a time, there was a very, very large tiger who had three cubs. Every day at sunset, she played with her cubs, jumping, fighting and rolling around, and when it was dark they went into their cave to sleep ... Hey. *(Nudges son)* I'm telling you the story. Don't fall asleep ...

SON: I'm not, I'm listening ...

FATHER: *(Continues)* One sunset in autumn, while hunting for food, the tiger was struck by a hunter's arrows, and barely got away with her life. Back home, unaware of her wounds, her cubs pounced on her with delight, and she played with them like nothing was wrong, jumping, fighting and rolling around. At night, they went into their cave. Encircled by her sleeping cubs, the tiger died at dawn. When her cubs awoke and found her dead, they were petrified, and ... *Hey*. Are you awake?

*The Son is fast asleep.*

FATHER: *(Gently raps son's head)* Hello, is anyone there ...? The boy fell asleep.

MOTHER: *(Offstage)* Yes, it's me! I'm home now ...!

*December 1925*

# ABOUT THE AUTHOR

**Ryūnosuke Akutagawa** (1892 – 1927), referred to frequently as "the father of the Japanese short story", was born in Tokyo midway through the Meiji Era – during which Japanese society underwent Western-influenced modernization at a frenetic pace, becoming a nascent superpower. His mother suffered from an indeterminate mental illness, and would die when her son was very young; the boy was adopted by his maternal uncle and aunt before his first birthday. (The surname by which we know him today comes from his maternal line.)

Akutagawa was admitted to Tokyo Imperial University with ease in 1913. There he studied English literature and began to write short fiction, attracting national attention (including praise from the greatest author of the day, Natsume Sōseki) in 1916 with his short story "The Nose". Impressively prolific, his influences and thematic preoccupations ranged widely, and he became known for his psychologically vivid, haunting, virtuoso style.

Beginning in the 1920s, his health began to decline, and he committed suicide at the age of thirty-five. He had written over 150 short stories and novellas, and eventually became one of the most widely translated Japanese writers. Famously, the Japanese master filmmaker Akira Kurosawa adapted Akutagawa's 1921 story "In a Grove" as the 1950 film *Rashōmon* (though the title and framing story derive from Akutagawa's 1915 story of the same name).

The Akutagawa Prize, founded in 1935 and named commemoratively, is today one of Japan's most prestigious literary awards.

# ABOUT THE TRANSLATOR

**Ryan Choi** lives in Honolulu, Hawai'i, where he was born and raised. He is an editor at the literary magazine *AGNI*. His work has appeared in *Harper's Magazine, The Nation, The New Criterion, The New Republic, Raritan, The Yale Review*, and other publications. This is his first book of translation.

## Selected Titles from Paper + Ink

**and the earth drank deep & Other Stories:**
**Winners of the Commonwealth Short Story Prize 2022**

**I Cleaned the – & Other Stories:**
**Winners of the Commonwealth Short Story Prize 2021**

**The Great Indian Tee and Snakes & Other Stories:**
**Winners of the Commonwealth Short Story Prize 2020**

**Emissaries: Stories and Reflections**
*Dean William Rudoy*

**Million-Story City: The Undiscovered Writings of Marcus Preece**
*Edited by Malu Halasa and Aura Saxén*

**Another Man**
*Leslie Croxford*

**The Dead**
*James Joyce*

**The Overcoat**
*Nikolai Gogol*
*Translated from the Russian by Constance Garnett*

**Bartleby, the Scrivener**
*Herman Melville*

**Independence Day & Other Stories**
*Pramoedya Ananta Toer*
*Translated from the Indonesian by Willem Samuels*

**In the Shadow of Death**
*Rūdolfs Blaumanis*
*Translated from the Latvian by Uldis Balodis*

**The Necklace & Other Stories**
*Guy de Maupassant*

PAPER + INK

**www.paperand.ink**